Little Flower Folks

This edition published 2025
by Living Book Press
Copyright © Living Book Press, 2025

ISBN: 978-1-76153-679-3 (hardcover)
         978-1-76153-691-5 (softcover)

First published in 1891.

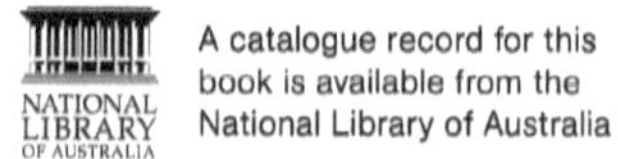

A catalogue record for this book is available from the National Library of Australia

Little Flower Folks

or Stories From Flowerland for the Home and School

Volume 1

by

Mara Louise Pratt-Chadwick

Contents

Introduction. 1

PART 1

I. – The Plant. 3
II. – The Root. 9
III. - The Stems. 15
IV. – The Leaves. 19
V. – The Flower. 27
VI. - Arrangement of Leaves and Flowers. 31
VII. - the Fruit. 40

PART 2

The Fairy Garland. 49
I. - Hepatica or Liverwort. 55
II. - Sanguinaria, or Blood-Root 63
III.- Trailing Arbutus. 71
IV. - Marsh Marigold and Anemones. 76
V - Buttercup, Dandelion, Coltsfoot. 86
VI. - Shad-blow or June-berry - Saxifrage. 93
VII. - Trillium. 97
VIII. - Adder's Tongue, or Dog-tooth Violet,
        and Bellwort or Wild Oat. 101
IX. – Columbine. 110

Introduction.

There is in children an innate love for flowers. No one so enthusiastically welcomes the springtime as do the children — no one else has time to welcome it, to no one else is it all so new and beautiful. Then why not nourish and cultivate this taste of the child for the flower world? Is it not as elevating, as worthy, as refining as the taste for dogs and cats, mice and men to which the ordinary reading book so sedulously caters?

Then the flower world is so full of beauty, so full of legend and lyric — and it is so free to us all! Let us in the springtime when the flowers are waking, and in the autumn when the flowers are closing their bright eyes in sleep, leave our hum-drum reading books and open out this big book of Nature to children — it is their book, it belongs to them because they seem to belong to it, because they understand it, because they love it. Why not bring to them what is their own — why should we, what right have we to keep them from their own?

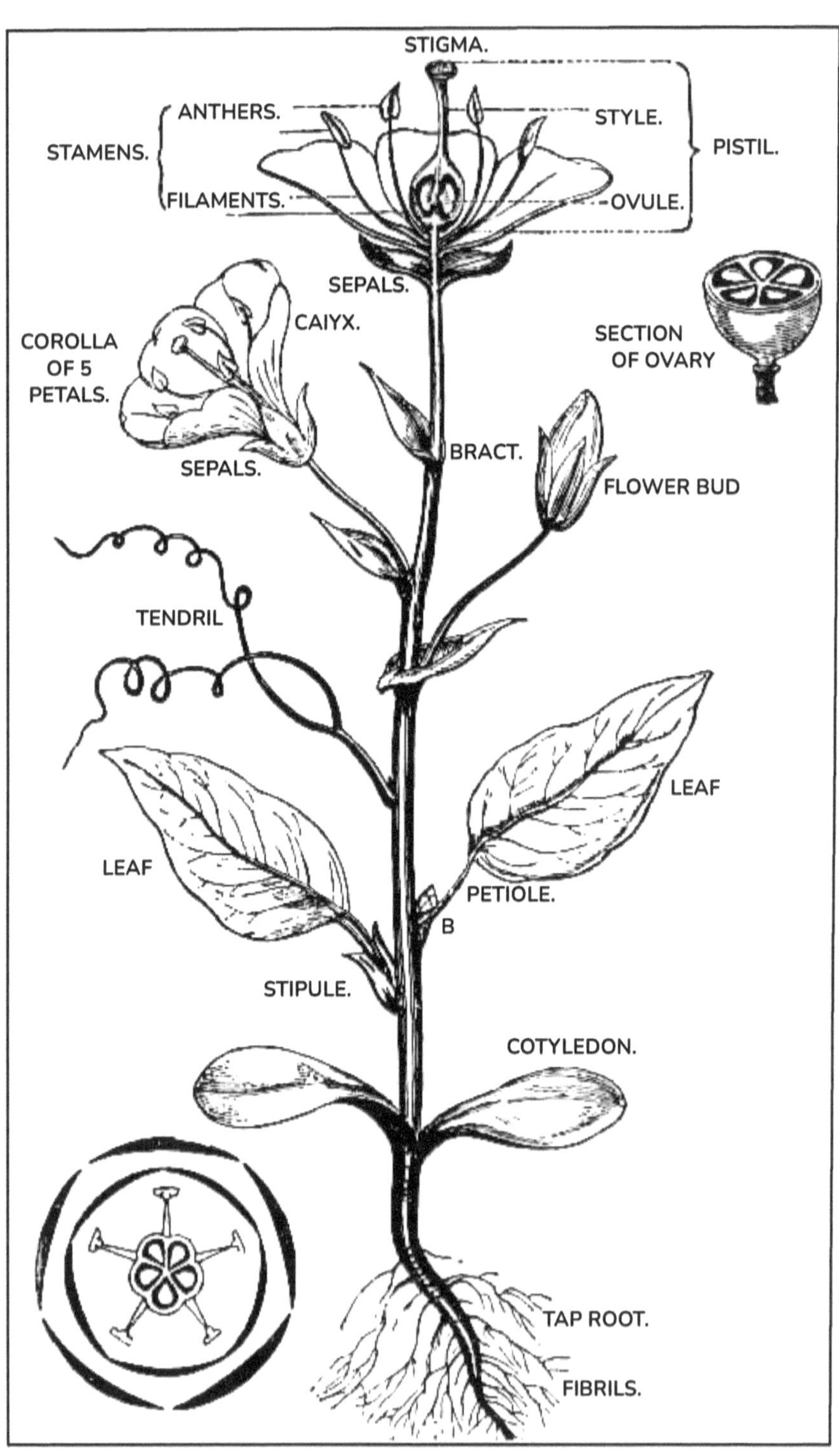

STIGMA.
ANTHERS.
STYLE.
STAMENS.
PISTIL.
FILAMENTS.
OVULE.
SEPALS.
CAIYX.
SECTION
OF OVARY
COROLLA
OF 5
PETALS.
SEPALS.
BRACT.
FLOWER BUD
TENDRIL
LEAF
LEAF
PETIOLE.
B
STIPULE.
COTYLEDON.
TAP ROOT.
FIBRILS.

PART I.

1. – The Plant.

root   *leaves*   *buds*
stems   *leaflet*   *blossom*
leaf   *flowers*   *seed-cradle*
                plantlet

"THE flowers are coming! The flowers are coming!" cried the children in a little country school one day at recess.

"O, I am so glad," answered the teacher.

"I thought these April showers must bring out the May flowers."

"Why, that's just what mamma said!" cried Alice, delighted and surprised that mamma and teacher should say exactly the same thing.

"Did she indeed?" answered the teacher, with a queer little smile. "Ask mamma for me how she supposes it ever happened."

"I suppose, children, if we wish to go out 'botanizing' by and by, as the big boys and girls down in the village do, we really ought to begin to be getting ready. A journey into Flower-land is like a journey into Europe; beautiful as it is, there is a certain amount of plain, hard work to be done before we are ready to start."

"Why can't we begin now and have it over with?" said

Harry. "That's the way I do with my wood-box. I hate wood-boxes; but if I must fill 'em, why I'd rather do it in the morning than to have the horrid things on my mind all play-time."

"You are a real philosopher, Harry!" laughed the teacher.

Harry looked puzzled and stuffed his hands hard into his pockets. But there was a kind, warm light in his teacher's eyes that told him that, whatever the big word meant, she wasn't making fun of him. And he was content.

"I don't know but Harry's plan is a good one," continued the teacher. "All those in favor of Harry's plan of beginning now and having it over with, say 'Aye!'"

"Aye! Aye! Aye! Aye! Aye! Aye!" came the hearty shout in reply.

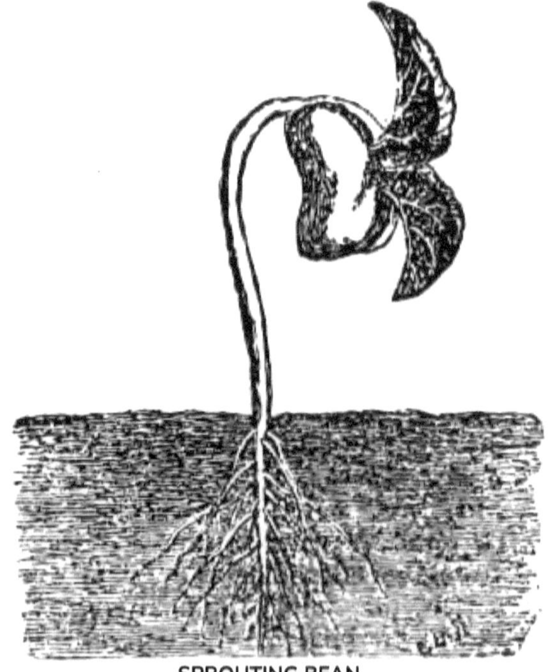

SPROUTING BEAN.

"All those opposed" —

Not a sound.

"I think there's no doubt it is a vote. Now for work. First of all, let us see what a plant has to do. It doesn't have geography lessons to learn, well enough that her children are out of mischief, busy at something. She, like all wise mothers, knows to be sure; but Mother Nature is happy and busy. Harry, tell me, if you plant a seed, what is the first thing that happens as far as you can see?"

"It begins to grow — to sprout."

"Yes, to grow; then we will say that the first work a plant has to do is to *grow*.

"You have all noticed that a plant is made of root, stem, and leaves. These are all a plant needs to make it grow even to the size of a tree; and if growing were all a plant had to do, very likely a *root*, a *stem*, and some *leaves* would be all we should ever see in any plant.

SNOW – DROP.

"But plants do have something else to do. By and by they have to *flower*. And later still while you are watching the beautiful flower, and admiring its rich color, in there among the green leaves, it is busy forming little seeds, rolling them away snugly in their little seed-cradles, telling them to take a good, long nap that they may be big and strong by and by to send out their own little plantlets and train them up into beautiful, tall plants.

"So we may say that the mission of the plant is:

a. to grow,

b. to flower,

c. to form seeds.

"And if it is an honest, busy little plant, think what a world of beauty it makes for us; and how happy it makes the people. And the best of all is that it never once thought of that when it was working away so patiently. I think that must be Mother Nature's reward to her children for 'well-doing.'"

ACORN AND CHESTNUT.

One pleasant day in October an acorn and a chestnut were lying side by side on the brown earth where they had fallen. "I hope I shall be safe in the ground before winter comes," said the acorn. "Snow and ice do not agree with me. In fact, if they come before I am under shelter they will kill me and it would be sad indeed, if so fine and large an acorn as I am should be lost; for I expect to become a great oak some time, and oaks, as you know, are the kings of the forest."

"Yes, I hope so, too," said the chestnut, "I want to be safe before winter comes. I would like to grow into a tree; for the swallows have told me that in all lands a strong, tall tree is thought to be one of the finest things in the world."

"Oh, chestnut trees are not much," said the acorn. "No one cares anything about them except the boys, who think it fun to climb up among their branches and shake down the nuts. For my part, if I were a tree, I shouldn't care to live just to please a few children; and I am sure it would make me very angry to see them eating the fruit which I had taken the trouble to bear."

"Well," said the chestnut, "every tree to its taste. Some trees would rather have their food liked by boys and girls than have it to be fit for nothing but pigs."

"What?" said the acorn, growing angry. "The oak is the noblest of all the trees. From its wood are made the great ships that go sailing over the ocean. It lives hundreds of years and gives shade to thousands of people, and homes to millions of birds; and if, as I heard a man say one day, 'great oaks from little acorns grow,' what a noble tree may be expected from such an acorn as I am!"

"But how will you be planted?" asked the chestnut.

"Oh, that's easy enough," answered the acorn. "Every day I feel myself sinking deeper and deeper into the ground; and when I am deep enough the wind will throw some fine rich earth over me, and there I shall lie snug and warm until spring.

"Then, after putting out two little green leaves, I shall

grow no more above ground for some time, but only keep spreading my roots and making them stronger. I shall grow slowly for years, until at last I shall spread out my branches for a great distance around, and become the king of the forest. Ah, how glad I am that I'm an acorn and not a chestnut!"

Just then a squirrel, who had been peeping at them from her nest in the hollow of a tree, jumped down and seized the chestnut in her little gray paws.

"Good-by," sneered the acorn, as she carried it away. "That's the last of *you*. But there is no great loss. You would have been only a chestnut tree, at the best. Chestnuts are good enough for squirrels."

But, when the squirrel had put the chestnut away in her nice little house, she sprang down again, seized the acorn and carried it up too.

"Hello," said the chestnut, "here we are together again. There is little hope now that either of us will ever become a tree. And, as matters stand, I cannot see that an acorn is very much better than a chestnut after all."

But the acorn said nothing.

II. – The Root.

radicle   iris   air-roots

plumule   turnip   plantlet

               cotyledons

IN order to live we have to eat and drink, and breathe in good air. So with the plant; with its roots it takes in what food it needs from the soil about it, with the stem it carries the food up to the plant above; and with its leaves it drinks in the air and sunlight.

Inside each seed, small as it is, there is already formed a little plantlet — that is, there are two tiny leaves and a little wee, wee root; all so small that you would need to take it out from the seed very carefully, and then would need a magnifying glass to see them with.

Take a bean for example. Soak it, and the shiny covering will shrivel away from the hard part inside. Examine that hard part. Do you see there are two parts to it — that they separate very easily? These are the cotyledons. And see again the two little points! One of those, called the *radicle*, will grow down into the ground, forming the root of the plant. The other one, called the *plumule*, will stretch up out of the earth into the sunlight to form leaves.

This radicle, or root, may take on different forms. The Iris, or Flag Plant, that boys so delight to wade into the water after, has an odd, irregular, knobby root; the common

YOUNG BEAN PLANT.

COUCH GRASS.

TAP ROOT OF TURNIP
AND CARROT.

BRANCHING ROOT.

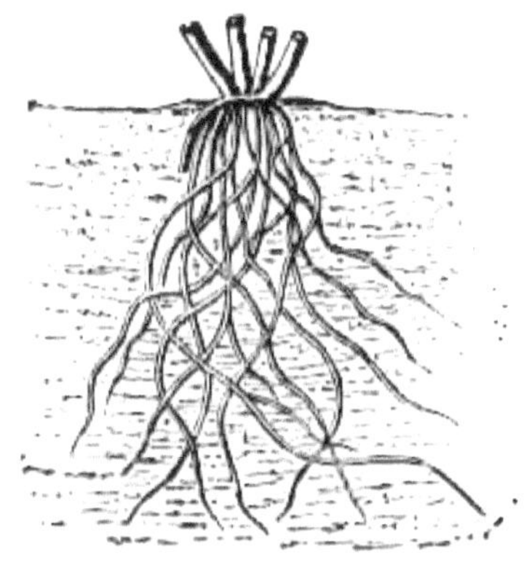

FIBROUS ROOT.

turnip plant has a cone-shaped root; other plants have roots like threads, reaching and spreading in all directions.

Sometimes, if a branch chances to be flattened down, so that for a long time it lies on the ground, it will send out little roots of its own, as if to say, "Since I cannot stand up in the bright sunlight with my brother branches, I may as well start a root here all of my own."

Another kind of root is the air-root. These you find growing all along the stems of certain climbing plants.

FLAGROOT.

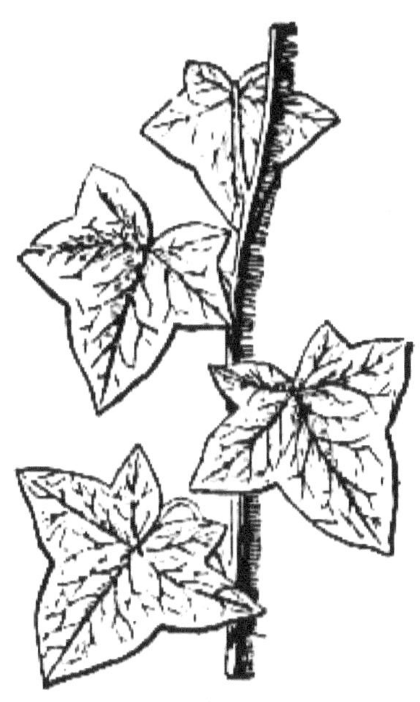

These little air-roots strike out from the vine, and seize upon the wall or tree upon which the vine is growing, and so hold it up in place.

HOW THE LEAVES CAME DOWN.

'LL tell you how the leaves came down,
The great tree to his children said:
"You're getting sleepy, Yellow and Brown.
Yes, very sleepy, little Red."

"Ah! begged each silly, pouting leaf,
"Let us a little longer stay;
Dear Father Tree, behold our grief;
'Tis such a very pleasant day,
We do not want to go away."

So, just for one more merry day
To the great tree the leaflets clung,
Frolicked and danced, and had their way,
Upon the autumn breezes swung,
Whispering, all their sports among.
"Perhaps the great tree will forget,
And let us stay until the spring,
If we all beg, and coax and fret."
But the great tree did no such thing —
He smiled to hear their whispering.

"Come, children all, to bed," he cried —
And, ere the leaves could urge their prayer,
He shook his head, and far and wide,
Fluttering and rustling everywhere,
Down sped the leaflets through the air.

I saw them; on the ground they lay,
Golden and red, a huddled swarm,
Waiting till one from far away,
White bedclothes heaped upon her arm,
Should come to wrap them safe and warm.

The great bare tree looked down, and smiled.
"Good night, dear little leaves," he said,
And from below each sleepy child
Replied, "Good night," and murmured,
"It is so nice to go to bed."

— SUSAN COOLIDGE.

III. – The Stems.

erect   *creeping*   *trailing*
decumbent *climbing*   *brier*
tendrils   *twining*   *thorn*

OTICE the different shapes of stems. Many of these forms, I have no doubt, you have drawn in your drawing books.

We will not stop in this little book to learn the names of these shapes. Keep that for by and by.

But these stems not only take on different shapes, but they have so many ways of growing.

There is the *erect* stem that grows straight up, or

CREEPING STEM

nearly so; the *decumbent* stem that lies along the ground
for a while, and then, as if it suddenly had grown strong
and had made up its mind not to be lazy, takes a turn
upward. Then there is the *trailing* vine that never gives

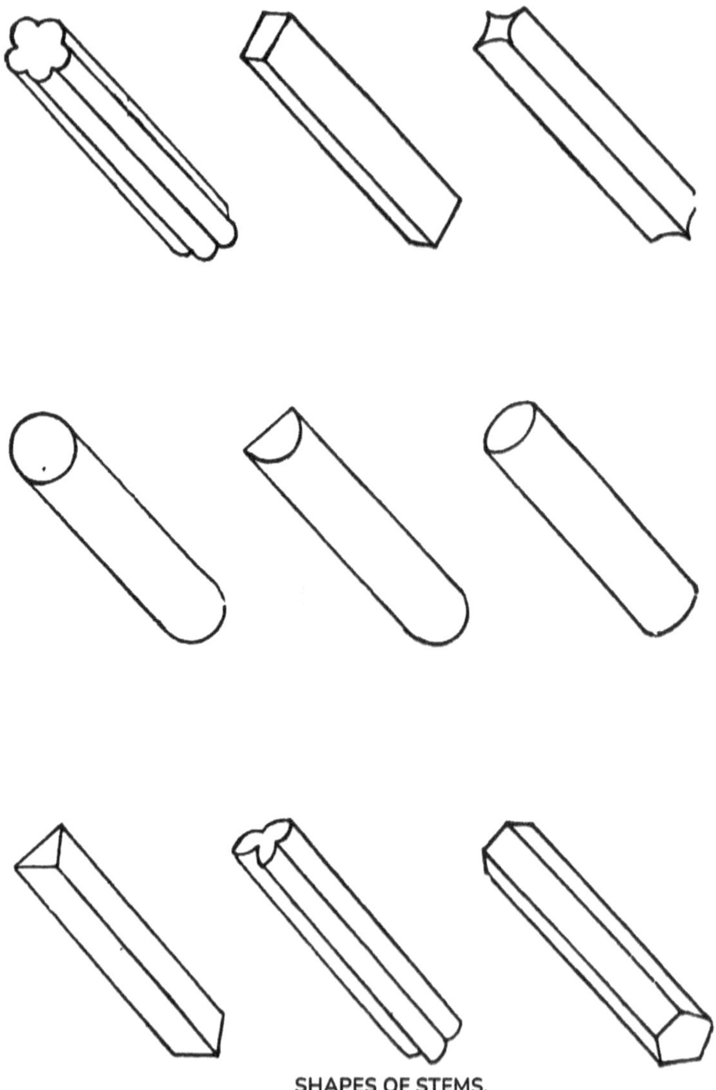

SHAPES OF STEMS.

up its first plan of lying abed forever but devotes itself to looking pretty and graceful as it lies, smiling up at the sun; then there is the *creeping* or running stem that not only has made up its mind to lie abed forever but, lest someone might insist on shaking it up into a standing position, has driven down, here and there, some little roots that hold it very firmly in place. Then there are the *climbing* stems that, although they don't quite like to lie forever on the ground, yet haven't quite strength enough to "stand alone," so fasten themselves around the erect stems of other plants; then there are the *twining* stems, like the climbers, except that I fancy they grow to love the brave erect stems upon which they climb, and so twine themselves about them.

There are other stems too. The comical little curls on the grape-vines – tendrils - are stems. Yes, and thorns and briers, stubborn, willful, aggressive little fellows - they too are stems.

THE KIND OLD OAK.

It was almost time for winter to come. The little birds had all gone far away, for they were afraid of the cold. There was no green grass in the fields, and there were no pretty flowers in the gardens. Many of the trees had dropped all their leaves. Cold winter, with its snow and ice, was coming. At the foot of an old oak tree, some sweet little violets were still in blossom. "Dear old oak," said they, "winter is coming; we are afraid that we shall die of the cold."

"Do not be afraid, little ones," said the oak. "Close your yellow eyes in sleep and trust to me. You have made me glad many a time with your sweetness. Now I will take care that the winter shall do you no harm."

So the violets closed their pretty eyes and went to sleep; they knew that they could trust the kind, old oak. And the great tree softly dropped red leaf after red leaf upon them until they were all covered over.

The cold winter came with its snow and ice, but it could not harm the little violets. Safe under the friendly leaves of the old oak, they slept and dreamed happy dreams until the warm rains of spring came and woke them again.

IV. – The Leaves.

variety *blade* *veins*
peculiar *foot-stalk* *vein lets*
genteel *stipules* *netted*
sullen *mid rib* *parallel*

SUCH a variety of leaves as there is! Every plant has its own peculiar leaves just as each of us has his own peculiar face. There are the long, narrow, genteel leaves like the long, narrow, genteel faces; the broad, happy leaves like the broad, happy faces; sometimes, too, there are the rough, coarse leaves like the rough, coarse faces;

LEAVES AND STIPULES.

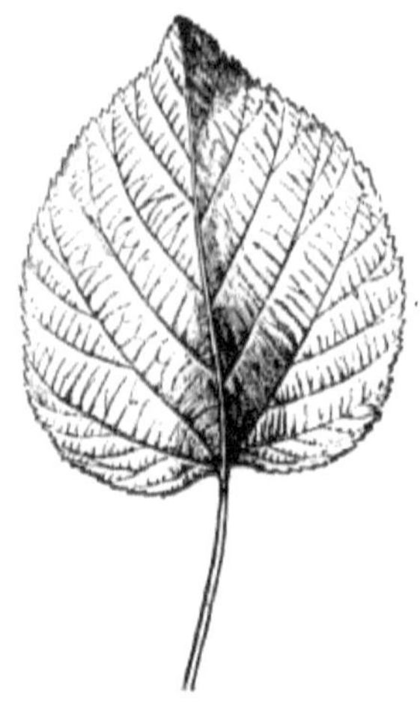

NETTED-VEINED LEAF.

PARALLEL-VEINED LEAF.

and the thick, heavy, sullen leaves like the thick, heavy, sullen faces. Plants and people are wonderfully alike!

Now, each leaf has a blade and a foot-stalk. There are also little stipules found at the base of the foot-stalk.

Up through the center of most leaves, you will find a mid-rib, and branching out from it, then dividing and subdividing, the veins and veinlets.

Such a leaf as that is called netted-veined because, as you see, the veins form a network.

Sometimes, however, you will find the mid-rib and the veins all running alongside each other from one end of the leaf to the other - parallel as the rails of a railroad track. Such leaves are called parallel-veined leaves.

As to the shapes of leaves, I hardly dare tell you how many there are lest you be discouraged! Here are the most common ones and the ones with the easiest names.

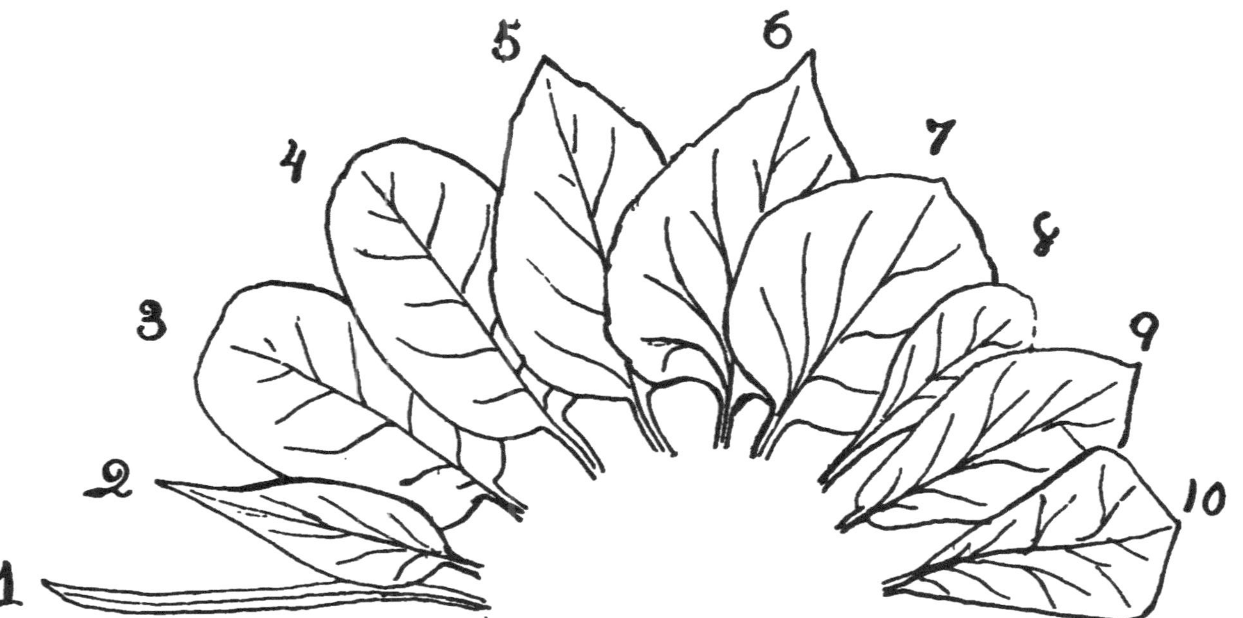

1. Linear - like straight lines. 2. Lance-shaped. 3. Oblong. 4. Oval. 5. Ovate.
6. Heart-shaped. 7. Round. 8. Spatulate. 9. Reversed-ovate (See 5). 10. Wedge-shaped.

Did you ever notice the difference in the edges of leaves? The six shown on the next page are the common kinds of edges.

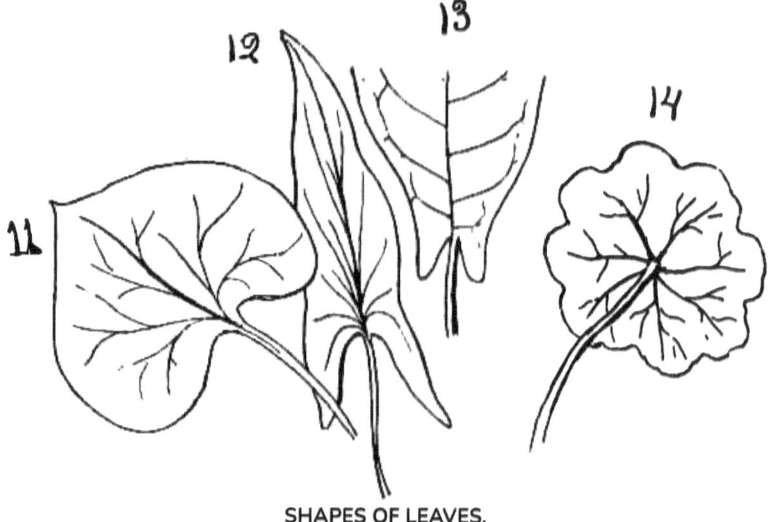

SHAPES OF LEAVES.

11. Kidney-shaped   12. Arrow-shaped.
13. Ear-shaped.   14. Shield-shaped.

All these are simple leaves, but sometimes leaves are so very jagged or so very much divided into parts all growing from one mid-rib that they are called compound leaves, and the little parts that make up the compound leaf are called leaflets, that is, little leaves (see illustration p24).

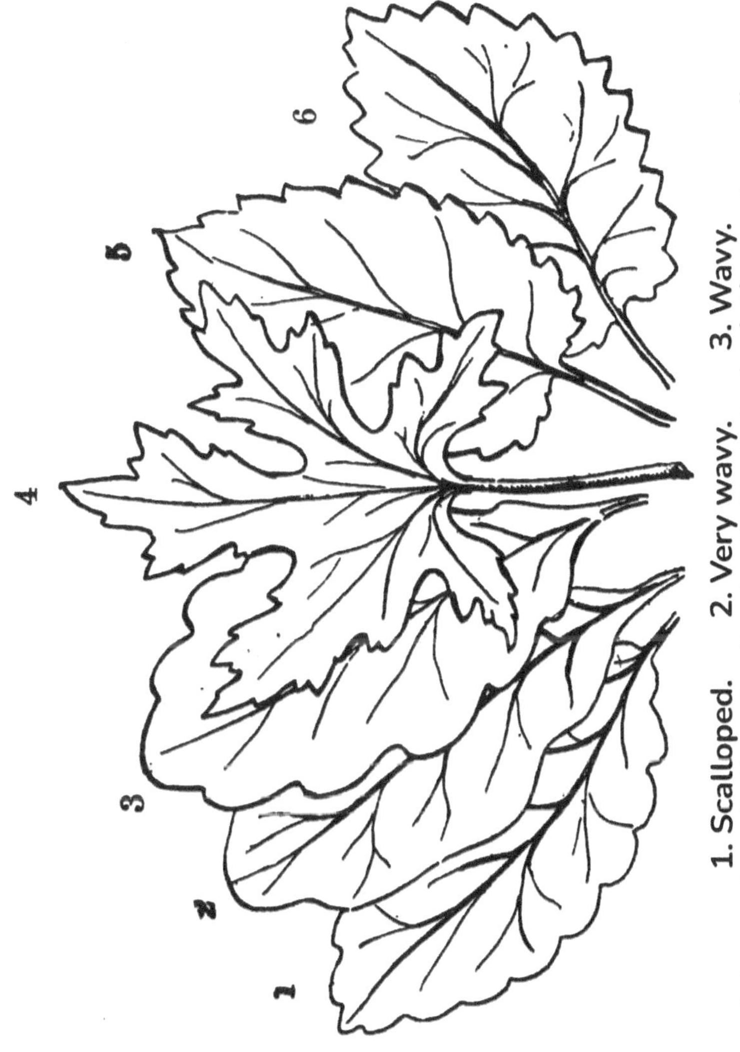

EDGES OF THE LEAVES.

23

COMPOUND LEAVES.

THE STORY OF THE MORNING - GLORY SEED.

MORNING – GLORY.

A little girl one day in the month of May dropped a Morning-glory seed into a small hole in the ground and said: "Now, Morning-glory seed, hurry and grow, grow, grow until you are a tall vine covered with pretty green leaves and lovely trumpet flowers." But the earth was very dry, for there had been no rain for a long time, and the poor wee seed could not grow at all. So, after lying patiently in the small hole for nine long days and nine long nights, it said to the ground around it: "O ground, please give me a few drops of water to soften my hard brown coat so that it may burst open and set free my two green seed-leaves, and then I can begin to be a vine!" But the ground said: "That you must ask of the rain."

So the seed called to the rain: "O rain, please come down and wet the ground around me so that it may give me a few drops of water. Then will my hard brown coat grow softer and softer until at last it can burst open and set free my two green seed-leaves and I can begin to be a vine!" But the rain said: "I cannot unless the clouds hang lower."

So the seed said to the clouds: "O clouds, please hang lower and let the rain come down and wet the ground around me so that it may give me a few drops of water. Then will my hard brown coat grow softer and softer until at last it can burst open and set free my two green seed-leaves and I can begin to be a vine!" But the clouds said: "The sun must hide first."

So the seed called to the sun: "O sun, please hide for a little while so that the clouds may hang lower and the rain come down and wet the ground around me. Then will the ground give me a few drops of water and my hard brown coat grow softer and softer until at last it can burst open and set free my two green seed-leaves and I can begin to be a vine!" "I will," said the sun, and he was gone in a flash.

Then the clouds began to hang lower and lower, and the rain began to fall faster and faster, and the ground began to get wetter and wetter, and the seed-coat began to grow softer and softer until at last open it burst! - And out came two bright green seed-leaves and the Morning-glory Seed began to be a Vine!

- MARGARET EITINGE

V. - The Flower.

corolla   *stamens*   *pistil*
petals   *pollen*   *style*
calyz   *anthers*   *stigma*
sepals   *filaments*   *seed cradle*

Now for the flower! - the only part of the plant we careless-eyed people often notice.

Here is a flower separated so that we may see it plainly. First of all, standing up like a flag-staff in the middle is the *pistil*.

Notice that the lower end of it is large and rounded. That is the seed-cradle, and inside it, by and by, are the little seeds containing the next year's plants.

The long erect part of the pistil is called the style, and the enlarged upper end is called the stigma.

FUCHSIA.

The pistil has, then, a seed-cradle, a style, and a stigma.

But what are all those thready things all around the pistil, looking somewhat like the pistil, and still *not* like it.

Those are the stamens. The long thready part is called the filament, and the enlarged parts at the upper ends that look so much, in the picture, like the stigma of the pistil, are the anthers. There is on these anthers a powdery

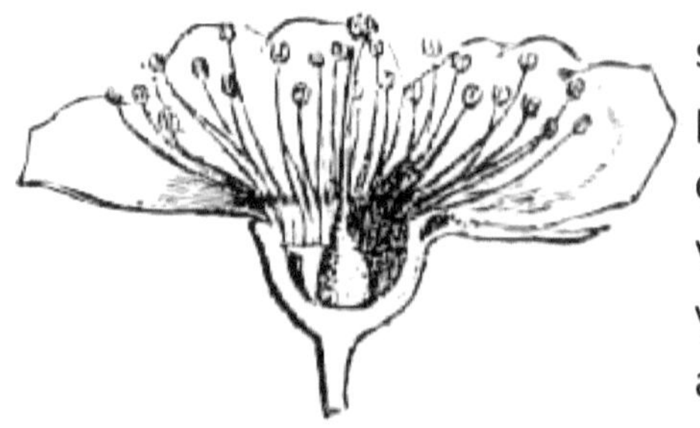

FLOWER OF PLUM.

stuff called pollen. This pollen rubs off easily enough, as your noses will often testify when you have been smelling a flower too closely.

Next we notice the broad, spreading part of the flower - the colored part - the part that arranges itself about the center of the flower in more or less of a wheel-shape. This is the corolla.

Sometimes this is all one unbroken wheel; then again it is divided into three, four, or five parts. These parts are then called the *petals*.

Below this and wrapped about it is a little green covering. You remember, there is first the bud, a little roundish bunch so carefully closed over by little green fingers. By and by these fingers begin to unclasp when lo, there peeps out the bright color of the corolla.

This green covering is the *calyx*, and its parts are called *sepals*.

And so you see, in speaking of a flower we mention *the sepals of the calyx; the petals of the corolla; the filaments and anthers of the stamens; and the seed-cradle, the style, and the stigma of the pistil.*

PARTS OF THE FLOWER.

28

THE ANXIOUS LEAF.

NCE upon a time a little leaf was heard to sigh and cry, as leaves often do when a gentle wind is about. And the twig said, "What is the matter, little leaf?"

And the leaf said, "The wind just told me that one day it would pull me off and throw me down to die on the ground!"

The twig told it to the branch on which it grew, and the branch told it to the tree. And when the tree heard it, it rustled all over and sent back word to the leaf, "Do not be afraid; hold on tightly, and you shall not go till you want to."

And so the leaf stopped sighing but went on nestling and singing. Every time the tree shook itself and stirred up all its leaves, the branches shook themselves, and the little twig shook itself, and the little leaf danced up and down merrily, as if nothing could ever pull it off. And so it grew all summer long till October.

And when the bright days of autumn came, the little leaf saw all the leaves around becoming very beautiful. Some were yellow, and some scarlet, and some striped with both colors. Then it asked the tree what it meant. And the tree said, "All these leaves are getting ready to fly away, and they have put on these beautiful colors because of joy."

Then the little leaf began to want to go too and grew very beautiful in thinking of it, and when it was very gay in color, it saw that the branches of the tree had no bright color in them, and so the leaf said, "O branches! why are you lead-color and we golden?"

"We must keep on our work-clothes, for our life is not done; but your clothes are for holiday, because your tasks are over," said the branches.

Just then, a little puff of wind came, and the leaf let go, without thinking of it, and the wind took it up and turned it over and over and whirled it like a spark of fire in the air, and then it dropped gently down under the edge of the fence among hundreds of leaves, and fell into a dream, and it never woke up to tell what it dreamed about.

VI. – Arrangement of Leaves and Flowers.

end-flower   *branch-flowers* *raceme*
corymb   *umbel*   *head*
spike   *catkin*   *spadix*
axillary   *opposite*   *whorled*
bracts   *alternate*

I WONDER if you ever noticed that flowers and leaves have as many different ways of arranging themselves as there are different kinds to arrange.

There is the unsocial little end-flower that grows up all by itself alone, with not even leaves to keep it company. And yet, it nods and smiles so pleasantly with all the other little end-flowers that one can hardly say it is unsocial after all.

Perhaps it is one of those flower-people who think it well to be on kind terms with everybody, and still be intimate with no one. Well, there are a good many other people who reason the same way. Perhaps they are right — who knows?

The very opposite of this kind of flower-people are those of the Spadix, the Spike, and the Head. These people seem to delight in cuddling as close together as possible — like so many snug little "bugs in a rug."

Then, in the Raceme, are the people that like to be

END FLOWER. – VIOLET.

HEAD. – CLOVER.

SPADIX OF ARUM.

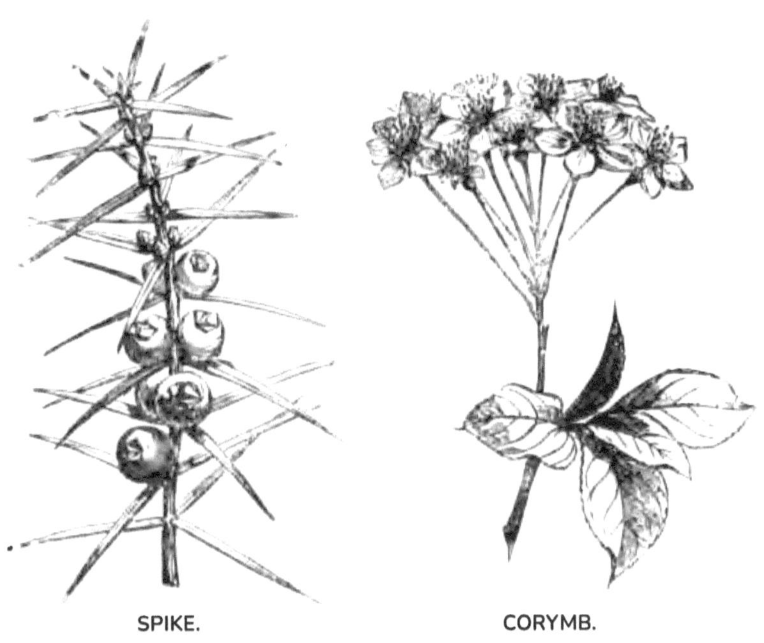

SPIKE.

CORYMB.

RACEME OF CURRANT.

UMBEL

near enough to be very neighborly, and still not quite so neighborly as the people of the Spike, the Spadix, and the Head.

Sometimes, too, flowers, starting at different places up and down the stem, like to stretch themselves up to be all on a level together. "We can talk so much better, and we can resist the storms so much better," they seem to say, "if we stand shoulder to shoulder." Such a cluster is a *corymb*.

Then there are the courteous little people who, starting all from the same place on the stem, stretch themselves out in such a manner as to give each other plenty of "elbow room" when, by and by, they find themselves, like the corymb, shoulder to shoulder. This makes a little extra growing for the outside rows of flower-people; but, as we said before, they are all courteous little people, not

AXILLARY FLOWER.

at all selfish or quarrelsome, and so are more than willing to work a little for the comfort of their little family circle. Such a group is called an *umbel*.

Other flower-people, liking to keep by themselves and close at home as well, are called *axillary* flowers because they peep out from the axils of the leaves, that is, in the angle formed by the leaf and the stem. I wonder what in the great world frightens them that, peeping out, they nestle down into their homes so close. Certainly, it is a very sunny, beautiful world; but perhaps its very large-ness may frighten them, or perhaps, seeing that they cannot reach very far out into it, they decide they might as well not reach out at all, but just settle down to enjoy the beauty as they see it from their own little homes.

But has this seemed an "extra hard lesson — extra long"? Perhaps it has; so you shall rest a while, and I will

CATKIN OF WILLOW.

tell you a story of a Catkin, that is, a little blossom that encloses itself in little, hard shells called *bracts*. This little catkin that I shall tell you about was called Pussy Willow, and the two little bracts were her little hood.

PUSSY WILLOW'S HOOD.

ALL winter, Pussy Willow had been shut up in her house by the brook; but one bright spring morning, she opened the door and stepped out. None of the flowers were up yet; the brook, the birds, the buds, and a few grass blades were the only friends she saw.

"Why, whom have we here?" asked the Brook in surprise, "Mistress Pussy Willow, as I live. Good morning, Pussy, you are up bright and early, but why do you wear that fur hood? Summer is coming, and every day grows warmer!"

"Oh, Mother Nature told me to keep it on, lest I get a toothache."

Everybody was glad to see Pussy. They all had something to say to her, but they were all curious to know why she had on that fur hood. Poor Pussy, she was tempted to take it off, they all said so much about it; but she didn't.

To make matters worse, Mr. Robin whispered some sly things to Pussy's friends, and the next morning when Pussy came out, the birds, the buds, the grass, and the brook began to shout, "Bald head, bald head, Pussy Willow has to wear a wig because she has no hair. Pussy Willow is a cheat."

Pussy felt very badly, but all she said was, "Wait and see."

One morning after this, everyone had a surprise. There was Pussy Willow with no fur hood on her head, but bright, golden curls dancing up and down in the breeze.

"Pussy is not a bald head. She has long, golden curls,"

LEAVES ALTERNATE.

cried all her friends, and mischief-making Mr. Robin went and hid his head for shame.

Now three more new words — easy ones they are — and we are done for this lesson.

Leaves arrange themselves in three ways. *Whorled* around the stem, so that it seems as if the stem must have been pushed through them; or in twos, just *opposite* each other on the stem; or *alternately*, up and down the stems, first one on one side, then another on the other side a little farther up.

TALKING IN THEIR SLEEP.

"YOU think I am dead,"
   The apple tree said,
     "Because I have never a leaf to show —
   Because I stoop,
   And my branches droop,
And the dull gray mosses over me grow!
   But I'm all alive in trunk and shoot;
 The buds of next May
 I fold away —
   But I pity the withered grass at my root."

   "You think I am dead,"
   The quick grass said,
"Because I have parted with stem and blade!
   But under the ground
   I am safe and sound
With the snow's thick blanket over me laid.
I'm all alive, and ready to shoot,
   Should the spring of the year
   Come dancing here —
But I pity the flower without branch or root."

   "You think I am dead,"
   A soft voice said,
"Because not a branch or root I own!
   I never have died,
   But close I hide,
In a plumy seed that the wind has sown,
Patient I wait through the long winter hours;
   You will see me again —
   I shall laugh at you then,
Out of the eyes of a hundred flowers."

—EDITH M. THOMAS, in St. Nicholas.

VII. – The Fruit.

EMEMBER we said the plant had three things to do:

To grow
To flower
To form seeds.

Along with seed-forming comes the making of fruit. Every plant has a fruit of some kind or other.

First it grows, then it flowers, and then comes the time for fruit forming. The corolla, the stamens, the pistils, and the calyx either fall off or shrivel up so that you never would know them, then the seed-cradle grows larger and larger — and we have the fruit.

There are so many different kinds of fruits. Indeed, why shouldn't there be when there are so many kinds of plants?

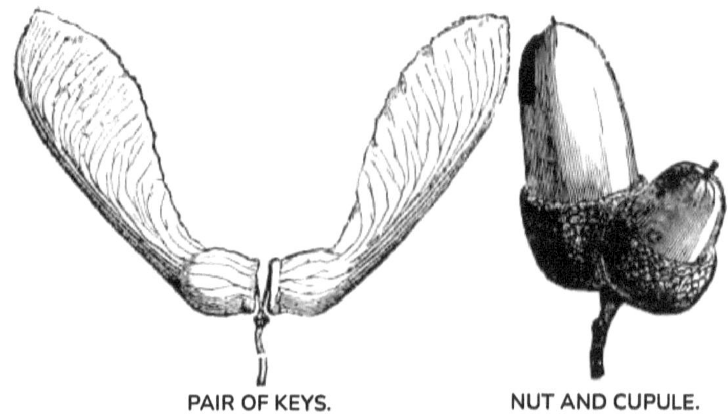

PAIR OF KEYS.   NUT AND CUPULE.

GOOSEBERRY

There are the *fleshy fruits* like the berries, the pears, the apples; the *dry* fruits like grain, nuts, and the keys that shower down from the Elm, the Maple, and the Ash trees; and the *stone fruits* like the plums, the cherries, and the peaches."

GRASS.

A SOUL IN GRASS AND FLOWERS.

ND what is so rare as a day in June?
    Then, if ever, come perfect days;
Then heaven tries the earth if it be in tune,
    And over it softly her warm ear lays;

Whether we look, or whether we listen,
We hear life murmur or see it glisten;
Every clod feels a stir of might,
An instinct within it that reaches and towers."

And groping blindly above it for light,
    Climbs to a soul in grass and flowers;
The flush of life may well be seen
    Thrilling back over hills and valleys:
The cowslip startles in meadows green,
    The buttercup catches the sun in its chalice,

42

And there's never a leaf nor a blade too mean
    To be some happy creature's palace."

Now the heart is so full that a drop overfills it,
We are happy now because God wills it;
No matter how barren the past may have been,
'Tis enough for us now that the leaves are green;
We sit in the warm shade and feel right well
How the sap creeps up and the blossoms swell;
We may shut our eyes, but we cannot help knowing
That skies are clear and grass is growing;
The breeze comes whispering in our ear,
That dandelions are blossoming near,
That maize has sprouted, that streams are flowing,
That the river is bluer than the sky,
That the robin is plastering his house hard by."
And if the breeze kept the good news back,
For other couriers we should not lack.

Joy comes, grief goes, we know not how
Everything is happy now,
    Everything is upward striving;
'Tis as easy now for the heart to be true
As for grass to be green, or skies to be blue, —
    'Tis the natural way of living.

                —LOWELL'S *Vision of Sir Launfal.*

THE VINE AND THE OAK.

A VINE was growing beside a thrifty oak, and had just reached that height at which it requires support. "Oak," said the vine, "bend your trunk so that you may be a support to me."

"My support," replied the oak, "is naturally yours, and you may rely on my strength to bear you up; but I am too large and too solid to bend. Put your arms around me, my pretty vine, and I will manfully support and cherish you, if you have an ambition to climb as high as the clouds."

"While I thus hold you up, you will ornament my rough trunk with your pretty green leaves and shining scarlet berries. We were made by the Master of Life to grow together, that by our union the weak may be made strong, and the strong render aid to the weak."

"But I wish to grow independently," said the vine; "why cannot you twine around me, and let me grow up straight, and not be a mere dependent on you?"

"Nature," answered the oak, "did not so design it. It is impossible that you should grow to any height alone; and if you try it, the winds and the rain, if not your own weight, will bring you to the ground."

"Neither is it proper for you to run your arms hither and thither among the trees. They will say, 'It is not my vine — it is a stranger — get thee gone; I will not cherish thee!' By this time thou wilt be so entangled among the different branches that thou canst not get back to the oak, and nobody will then admire thee, or pity thee."

"Ah, me," said the vine, "let me escape from such a destiny;" and she twined herself around the oak, and they grew and flourished happily together.

THE SECRET.

We have a secret, just we three,
The robin and I and the sweet cherry tree
The bird told the tree, and the tree told me,
And nobody knows it but just we three.

But of course, the robin knows it best,
Because he built the — I shan't tell the rest;

And laid the four little — somethings in it —
I am afraid I shall tell it every minute.

But if the tree and the robin don't peep,
I'll try my best the secret to keep;
Though I know when the little birds fly about,
Then the whole secret will be out.

—STEVENSON.

A BOUQUET OF SPRING VIOLETS.

After the slumber of the year,
The woodland violets reappear;
All things revive in field and grove,
And sea and sky; but two, which move
And form all others, life and love.

—SHELLEY.

REVIEW.

WONDER if you are ready to tell something about each word in this table. If you are, I am sure you are ready to go out into the fields with your teacher and do just what your big brothers and sisters do at the High School — "analyze flowers".

People who had charge of the schools used to think that all these pleasant things about the flowers, the stars, the rocks, and the animals must be kept hidden away from pupils until they were "grown up." But we are beginning to learn nowadays that little people are just as wide awake to the beautiful things in the world as "grown-up" people are — indeed, they are often a great deal more awake.

45

<u>**A PLANT IS MADE UP OF.**</u>

Root   Stem   Leaves

<u>**WHAT PLANTS DO.**</u>

Plants grow.   Plants flower.
Plants form seeds from which new plants grow.

<u>**PARTS OF A FLOWER.**</u>

Calyx, with its sepals   Pistil, with its style and
Corolla, with its petals   stigma
Stamens, with its filament   Ovary, or seed-vessel
   and anthers   Pollen

<u>**THE PLANTLET HAS.**</u>

Cotyledons   Radicle   Plumule

<u>**ARRANGEMENTS OF LEAVES.**</u>

Opposite   Alternate   Whorled

<u>**KINDS OF STEMS.**</u>

Upright   Creeping or   Twining
Decumbent   Running   Thorns and
Trailing   Climbing   Briers

<u>**PARTS OF LEAVES.**</u>

Blade   Veins   Stipules
Ribs   Foot-stalks

<u>**VEINING OF LEAVES.**</u>

Netted-veined
Parallel-veined

KINDS OF LEAVES.

Simple   Compound

SHAPES OF LEAVES.

Linear	Heart	Kidney
Lance	Round	Arrow
Oblong	Spatulate	Ear
Oval	Reversed-ovate	Shield
Ovate	Wedge-shaped	

EDGES OF LEAVES.

Saw-toothed	Scalloped	Very wavy
Dentate	Wavy	Jagged

ARRANGEMENT OF FLOWERS.

End-flowers	Branch-flowers	Raceme
Corymb	Umbel	Head
Spike	Catkin	Spadix

FRUITS.

Fleshy	Dry	Stone

And now our "work" is done. Now we are ready for the "play" part of flower study. "It hasn't been so very 'dry' after all, has it, Harry?" But the flowers have come and are ready to speak for themselves. And we are ready to greet them!

THE LITTLE BROWN SEED IN THE FURROW

A little brown seed in the furrow
        Lay still in its gloomy bed,
While violets blue and lilies white
        Were whispering overhead.
They whispered of glories strange and rare,
Of glittering dew and floating air,
Of beauty and rapture everywhere,
        And the seed heard all they said.

Poor little brown seed in the furrow,
        So close to the lilies' feet,
So far away from the great glad day,
        Where life seemed all complete!
In her heart, she treasured every word,
And she longed for the blessings of which she heard;
For the light that shone and the air that stirred
        In that land so wondrous sweet.

The little brown seed in the furrow
        Was thrilled with a strange unrest;
A warm, new life beat tremblingly
        In the tiny, heaving breast.
With her two small hands clasped close in prayer,
She lifted them up in the darkness there,
Up, up, through the dark, toward sun and air,
        Her folded hands she pushed.

O little brown seed in the furrow,
        At last you have pierced the mold;
And quivering with a life intense,
        Your beautiful leaves unfold.
Like wings outspread for upward flight,
And slowly, slowly, in dew and light,
A sweet bud opens — till, in God's sight,
        You wear a crown of gold.

                        — IDA W. BENHAM.

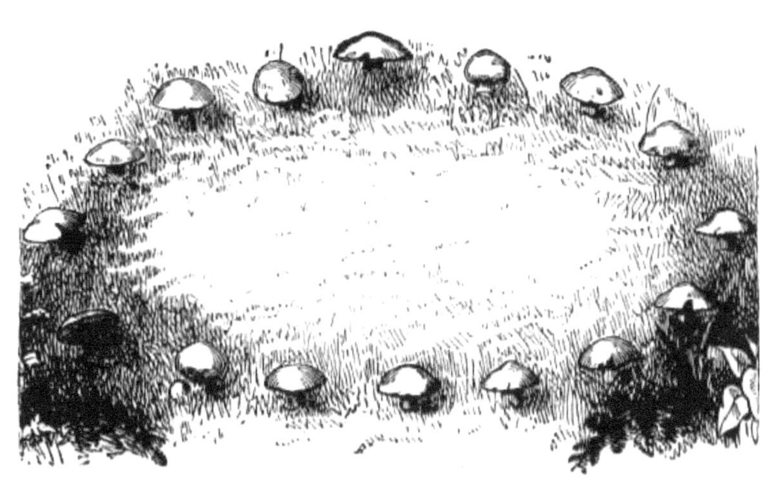

PART II.

The Fairy Garland.

N the good old times, as our grandpapas and our grandmamas like to say, people believed as truly that there were fairies as that there were boys and girls; and in some parts of Scotland and Old England there are, here and there, people who still believe in them to this day.

Many are the tales these people will tell of belated travelers who, passing through the great, broad moorlands at midnight, were seized upon by the little people and carried off to join the "fairy dance," or, as they call it, the "pixy dance."

"My little lad," said a man traveling through a rural English village, "what is this delicate white flower I see everywhere climbing up over the fences and hedges?"

"We calls 'em Pixies," answered the little fellow.

"Pixies!" exclaimed the gentleman, not expecting that answer. "Why do you call them that?"

"The Pixies are fond of them," answered the lad.

"Because they are white, like the Pixies," suggested another lad.

"O, do not touch them!" cried another, as he bent to gather the beautiful flowers. "The fairies will carry you off if you do!"

"Yes, yes, you'll surely be Pixey-led."

FOXGLOVE.

This plant then, the Stitchwort, or as the children call it, the Snapper or Snapjack, is one of the many plants believed by these simple folk to belong to the fairies.

This is by no means the only plant that the fairies claim. There are many, many more in this "Fairy Garland."

Another plant, Fairy Butter, is found in the mining regions, showing, of course, that the fairies live about the mines. One honest old miner told a traveler, with all the earnestness possible, that when the damp rises from these mines at night, the little people are heard to make strange noises — such knocking! Such hammerings! And the Fairy Butter-plant rocks back and forth, back and forth, and has been known to groan outright. All because the fairy folks do not like the heavy damp.

Of course, the toadstool belongs to the Fairy Garland. On pleasant nights the fairies sit or dance upon the tops of these; or, if there should come a sudden fall of rain, then the fairies huddle together beneath them. I once heard of an old village gardener who declared that he had actually seen the fairies holding a toadstool, umbrella fashion, over their fairy queen as she tripped home in the rain.

Then there is the Foxglove, by some said to have been once the Folks'-glove, that is, the glove of the "little folks." Others, however, believe the word glove came from the old word *gleow*, which means music, and that the little bell-like flowers were used for bells to make fairy music.

In a book which tells of the old English customs and beliefs of the people long ago, the author says: "It was believed that the 'Fairy Kingdom' was in Devonshire. A terrible fairy war followed. King Oberon was dethroned and his enemies were declared conquerors."

Before this sad battle, the fairies held a grand banquet.

> "A little mushroom, that was now grown thinner
> By being one time shaven for the dinner,"

served for a table. The dainty covering was of pure white rose-leaves; the trenchers of "little silver Spangles"; the salt, "the small bone of a fishe's backe"; the bread, "the milke-white kernells of the hazelnut": -

> "The cupboard, suiteable to all the rest,
> Was, as the table, with like cov'ring drest;
> The ewre and bason were, as fitting well,
> A perriwinckle and a cockle-shell;
> The glasses, pure and thinner than we can
> See from the sea-betroth'd Venetian,
> Were all of ice, not made to overlast
> One supper, and betwixt two Cowslipps cast."

And then we read of a little fairy, who, "cladd in a sute of rush," a "monkeshood flower serving for a hatt, and under a cloake of the spider's loome," brought in the bottles — every bottle was a "cherry-stone": -

> "To each a seed pearle served for a screwe,
> And most of them were fill'd with early dewe;
> Some choicer ones, as for the king most meet,
> Held mel-dew, and the honey-suckles sweet."

"The fairies had even their musicians, whose hautboys were of syves (i.e., chives): -

> "Excepting one, which pufte the player's face,
> And was a chibole, serving for the base."
> Then came the service. The first dishes were:

"In white broth boylde, a cramméd grasshopper;
The udder of a mouse two hornett's leggs;
Instead of olyves, cleanly pickl'd sloes;
Then of a batt were serv'd the petty-toes
Three fleas in souse; a cricket from the bryne;
And of a dormouse, last, a lusty chyne."

Truly a most dainty banquet.

WHAT ROBIN TOLD.

How do the robins build their nests?
Robin Redbreast told me.
First, a wisp of amber hay
In a pretty round they lay,
Then some shreds of downy floss,
Feathers too, and bits of moss,
Woven with a sweet, sweet song,
This way, that way, and across,
That's what robin told me.
Where do the robins hide their nests?
Robin Redbreast told me.
Up among the leaves so deep,
Where the sunbeams rarely creep;
Long before the winds are cold,
Long before the leaves are gold,
Bright-eyed stars will peep and see
Baby robins, one, two, three;
That's what robin told me.

— GEO. COOPER.

HEPATICA.

All the woodland path is broken
    By warm tints along the way,
        And the low and sunny slope
Is alive with sudden hope,
When there comes the silent token
    Of an April day—
        Blue hepatica!

I. – Hepatica or Liverwort.

ND now we are really to begin analyzing flowers. The drudgery of learning new words and names is all done. Now for the play-work!

How many succeeded in finding the *low herb* with the *three-lobed leaf and one little purplish flower at the end of a scape or naked stem*?

Johnny, Emma, Ella, Frank! Well done. And were you able to recognize them from the picture we had of them yesterday? Now we were all to bring a knife, a bit of magnifying glass, and some tiny strips of court plaster.

And, by the way, children — this has nothing to do with botany, to be sure — but did you ever hear why this is called Court Plaster? Long ago, when Charles I was king, it was the fashion among the court ladies to decorate their faces with bits of this plaster cut in shapes of crescents, rings, hearts, crosses, stars, etc. And in our own country, before the Revolution, these little patches of court plaster were worn as political emblems. The Whig ladies wore their patches on the *right* side of their faces, and the Tory ladies wore their patches on the *left* side. Just as now you often see before election the Republicans wearing one kind of badge, and the Democrats another kind. But now let us give our attention to this little plant with its *three-lobed leaves* and its *one flower at the end of a scape*.

First of all, let us write its name at the head of our papers:

HEPATICA OR LIVERWORT.

"Plants, like people, belong in families. Sometimes the families are large, sometimes they are small. Mr. Smilax, for example, is a lone bachelor with neither 'kith nor kin.'"

"As in a family of people, there are certain family 'traits' that are easily recognized in each member; and sometimes the faces are very much alike. Still, you would never be puzzled to distinguish one from the other, I think."

"Now, this plant we are to analyze today belongs to a large family called the

CROWFOOT FAMILY.

"In all plants belonging to this family, you will find - with one or two exceptions of which we may speak later: -
   1. *Compound or much-parted leaves*
   2. *No stipules*
   3. *Many pistils*
   4. *Many stamens*
   5. *Parts of the flower all separate and inserted on the receptacle.*"

"These five family traits we will keep here on the blackboard for reference. Who knows but we may be introduced to every member of this family before the season is over."

"In this particular flower, Harry, describe the leaf."

"The leaves of the Hepatica or Liverwort are three-parted. Some of them are reddish. They are on foot-stalks and grow in bunches from the root of the plant. There are no stipules. They are netted-veined."

"Describe the stem, Ella."

"The stem is a scape; that is, there are no leaves up and down its length."

"And the flower, Annie?"

"Outside is a little calyx of three sepals—"

"It is little wonder, Annie, that you called that the calyx; but look sharply. You will see those are not sepals — that they are really a little below the flower and are not at all connected with it. Really, these little sepal-like things are *a little whorl of tiny leaves just below the flower.*"

"Then there is no calyx!"

"Certainly, something is lacking! - Either there are no sepals or no petals."

"No sepals!" cried Harry; "for here are the petals pink as can be."

"Again our eyes deceive us, Harry. These very pink petals are, so the botanists tell us, the sepals. Remember this; for quite often as you go on, you will read in the botany of 'petal-like calyxes' or 'sepals colored like a corolla.'"

"What of the stamens, Willie?"

"Ever so many stamens!"

"More than twelve, as we read in the description of the Crowfoot Family, do you think?"

"O, yes; I've counted more than twelve already."

"And the pistil?"

"More than one."

"Yes; and in this flower that has long ago 'gone to seed,' as we say, the pistils have left little sharp-pointed achenes."

"There are two kinds of Hepaticas quite common in our country. In the East and North, we have this kind - with *three roundish-lobed leaves.* Farther west, we should find these *lobes sharper pointed and numbering either three or five.*"

"Why did this plant get the name of Liverwort? And what does Hepatica mean?"

"That's right, Harry. As far as possible, find out the 'why' of everything. Now as to the name of this plant, some say it is because the leaf is three-lobed like a liver; others say because its old leaves are liver-colored. At any rate, long, long ago, it was used as a remedy for all sorts of 'liver complaints' because its leaves were liver-shaped. In the same way, these simple people used another plant which chanced to have heart-shaped leaves for all sorts of heart diseases; the Celandine, because it had yellow juice, was the cure-all for jaundice; the herb-dragon, because it was spotted and striped, was the remedy for snake bites. This method of medical treatment was called the 'Doctrine of Signatures' — every herb having its own sign by which it could speak to man and tell its mission, if only man were wise enough to hear and understand."

CROWFOOT FAMILY.
Compound or much-parted leaves.
No stipules.
Many pistils and stamens.
Parts of the flower all separate and inserted on the receptacle.

HEPATICA.
A calyx-like whorl of leaves.
No calyx.
One blossom at the end of a scape.
Three-lobed leaves at the root.

"For tomorrow's lesson, I want you to bring a certain delicate white flower plant, the juice of which will stain your hands, O, so red!"

LEGEND OF THE AMBROSIA.

NCE upon a time, the Emperor of China, walking about in the quiet groves, came suddenly upon two women, one young, one very old.

To his astonishment, he saw that the younger woman was whipping the old, bent woman. "Shame upon you!" thundered the Emperor. "Do you not know that in our country respect for old age is counted one of the greatest virtues? How dare you thus abuse your old mother!"

"I myself am the mother," answered the younger-appearing woman. "This is my daughter, and justly does she deserve punishment. That I look younger than she is because I have eaten of the Ambrosia that gives perpetual youth."

"Perpetual youth!" exclaimed the Emperor. "Tell me, where is it to be found — how does it look? I myself am growing old. O, gladly would I be young again — young and strong and fit again to govern my country as once I did."

Of course, it was in a far, far country, and only after passing great rivers and climbing great mountains could the plant be found. But the Emperor was not discouraged. "If on the face of the earth that plant lives, it shall be mine," said he.

Accordingly, a faithful servant was dispatched for it with promises of untold wealth and honor should he return with even one branch of it to his country.

The faithful servant set out on his perilous journey, accompanied by many attendants. After weeks and weeks of tedious travel, at length, a hill was found covered thick with the wonderful plant.

A goodly amount was gathered, you may be sure— enough to make half the kingdom young. But alas! in the morning when the travelers awoke, the plant had withered, every branch. And more than that, every root had disappeared from the hillside.

No, not every root. Away down a steep precipice was just one plant.

"We must get that for our Emperor," said the servant.

"I will not risk my life for it," said one of his followers.

"Nor I."

"Nor I."

"Nor I," - said the others.

"But it must be had, and I myself will climb down for it."

Slowly and carefully, he made his way down the rocky steep. Suddenly, his grasp upon the bits of shrubs growing out here and there between the rocks gave way. Down, down he fell — so far down in the deep ravine that only a dark spot could be distinguished among the rugged rocks, where his crushed and bleeding form lay.

"Poor fool, he's dead!" said one cold-hearted attendant.

"Nay, not poor fool; rather faithful-hearted servant of our Emperor," answered another.

"But see! There rises a bird — a white bird! The stork — the immortal bird!"

Reverently, the attendants watched the beautiful white bird soar higher and higher, until lost to sight in the great blue sky.

"Truly it was the fairy messenger," said they, "come to bear the faithful soul to the realms of immortality."

And, turning slowly away, they returned to their own country to tell the story to the waiting Emperor; and to this time, the anniversary of the day is kept by the simple, devoted people, who gather upon the hillsides in the warm summer sunlight to bless the fairies for their goodness, and to watch for another appearance of the 'immortal bird,' the messenger of the fairies.

THE SWEET RED ROSE.

"Good morrow, little rose-bush,
    Now prithee, tell me true,
To be as sweet as a red rose
    What must a body do?"

"To be as sweet as a red rose,
    A little girl like you
Just grows, and grows, and grows,
    And that's what she must do."

— JOEL STACY.

11. Sanguinaria, or Blood-Root.

ND have we today the plant with the white flower and the blood-red juices?" Alice has found it surely, if I am to judge from the color of her hands. Indeed, they are as stained as Shakespeare tells us were Lady Macbeth's. However, a little water will remove these stains; while, if I remember rightly, Lady Macbeth feared that "all the perfumes of Arabia could not cleanse her little hand."

"I know what you mean! I've read that story!" cried Harry.

"I believe you've read everything, Harry," replied the teacher, her face brightening as some way it always did when Harry spoke. "Tell us the story, my boy. You don't know what a joy it is to have children in school that read and think."

"And ask 'why?'" piped up another little lad, anxious that Harry should not get all the praise.

"Yes, and ask *why*," answered the teacher, laughing at the boy's earnestness. "You always do that, dear; and you know I like it in you.

"Now the story, Harry. Just a few sentences — just enough to wake up our curiosity and make us want to read it for ourselves."

"Macbeth and Lady Macbeth plotted to kill the good

King Duncan so that they might get the throne for them-selves. They succeeded, to be sure; but they were far from happy. They had to murder first this one and then that one, in order to keep their secret.

"Everybody they thought who was likely to tell or was likely to get the throne away from them, they would kill. By and by, the ghosts of these murdered people began to haunt Macbeth and Lady Macbeth. Lady Macbeth had terrible dreams. She would wander up and down the great halls of the castle, crying out and trying to rub the blood-stains from her hand. By and by, she died; and Macbeth, so tired of life that he didn't much care whether he lived or not, went into battle with Macduff, a man he had 'most foully wronged,' and was killed by him."

"O, what a bad king!" cried Allie, whose wide-awake imagination always saw the story as "truly true."

"He grew to be pretty bad," answered Harry, with a shake of his head; "but he wasn't so very bad at first. Father told me that the object Shakespeare had in mind in writing that play was to show how, little by little, Macbeth grew to be a wicked man. Father says nobody ever gets to be bad all at once."

"I shall always think of Lady Macbeth when I see this flower, I know I shall," said Allie, with a real sigh, looking ruefully at her hands as if she were Lady Macbeth herself.

"Let's begin at once to examine the flower," laughed the teacher, "that we may get Allie's mind off this tragedy of Macbeth. First of all, I must tell you, this plant, called Sanguinaria or Blood-root, belongs to the

BLOOD-ROOT

POPPY FAMILY.

Yes, it is a little sister of those pretty, crinkly poppies that grow in the gardens. The poppy family has five 'family traits.'

1. *A bitter juice, white, red, or sometimes colorless.*
2. *Alternate leaves.*
3. *Flowers remarkable for having two sepals, and (Blood-root excepted) four petals.*
4. *Flowers short-lived.*
5. *Many stamens — one pistil with many seeds.*

Now in this flower — the Blood-root — you will notice first that the leaves and flowers never grow on the same stem; but from every joint of the foot-stalk, one large,

POPPIES.

round leaf rises, and one tall scape with its one terminal flower.

It will be rather difficult to dry this flower because its petals drop so easily; and then, too, the whole plant turns black as ink when dried.

No one brought a root of this plant. Did anyone see the root? It would be well always to examine that part of the plant. Sometimes it is very necessary to know about it in order to trace the plant to its right family.

"I saw the root, and it was like the picture we had of a tuberous root, I am sure."

"Yes, the root is tuberous. I am glad you noticed it."

Notice that the petals of this poppy are smooth — not crumpled. Another difference from all its sisters is that its bud does not nod. These points, together with its eight to twelve petals and its red juice, are perhaps all we need to note today. Perhaps you will like to know that just as its sister, the yellow-juiced Celandine, was supposed to be a remedy for jaundice, so this Blood-root was supposed to have the power to stop the flow of blood.

POPPY FAMILY.

Milk-white, red, yellow, or colorless juice. - Alternate leaves. - Flowers short-lived. - Two sepals. - Four petals (except in Blood-root). - Many stamens. - One many-seeded pistil.

BLOOD-ROOT

Eight to twelve petals — not crumpled. - Red juice. - Bud does not nod. - Tuberous root.

For the next lesson, let us find a trailing plant with little *clusters of very sweet-scented pink and white flowers.*

"O, I know what that is!"

"So do I!"

"And I!"

"And I!"

"Who knows the kind of leaves it has — the number of petals — the shape of the pistil — or the number of the stamens?

What careless-eyed people we are to be sure! We have seen this trailing plant every spring of our lives and never noticed anything but that it was pink-flowered and sweet-smelling!"

POPPIES IN THE WHEAT

Along Ancona's hills, the shimmering heat,
    A tropic tide of air with ebb and flow,
    Bathes all the fields of wheat until they glow
Like flashing seas of green which toss and beat
Around the vines.
The poppies lithe and fleet
    Seem running, fiery torchmen, to and fro
    To mark the shore.
The farmer does not know
That they are there. He walks with heavy feet,
    Counting the bread and wine by Autumn's gain,
    But I—I smile to think that days remain
Perhaps to me in which, though bread be sweet
    No more, and red wine warm thy blood in vain,
I shall be glad remembering how the fleet
Lithe poppies ran like torchmen with the wheat.

                —H. H.

STORY OF THE TULIP.

EAR a pixy-field in Devonshire, there lived an old woman who was very fond of flowers. Such a beautiful garden as she had! And such lovely beds of tulips! So delighted were the pixies with this garden that they used often to carry their pixie-babies there and sing them to sleep.

Often, at midnight, the sweetest strains of music would float up to the old woman's bedchamber. "Fairy music of course," said she. "Who could doubt it?" And the tulips, too, would sway back and forth, keeping time to the sweet melody.

As soon as the babies were asleep, away would the

pixie-mothers hasten to join the pixie dance, never for-getting, when the first streak of light shot across the sky, to come back for their babies sleeping so snugly in the beautiful tulip blossoms.

And so fragrant and large and queenly did the tulips grow that the good woman would never allow one of them to be plucked from its stem.

At length the owner of the garden died. And her son, a coarse, rough fellow, full of contempt for all such fool-ish notions about fairies, ploughed up the tulip bed and planted it full of parsnips. "No pixy-beds for me," sneered he; "I'll have parsnips to eat."

Of course, the pixies were angry enough. "Coarse fel-low!" said they, "he cares for nothing but to eat!"

And so, breathing upon the parsnips, they withered away, and never was the man able to make any sort of vegetables grow on that bit of land. Proof positive, was it not, that the good old mother was right, and that the fairies did put their babies to sleep nightly in the beauti-ful tulip bed?

And more than that, it was soon proved that the pixies knew where their good friend was buried. For at midnight often there was heard sweet music about her grave; and though no one took any care of the spot where she lay buried, no weeds grew there, and every day there sprang up the most beautiful flowers — real pixy flowers too — that no one could doubt who saw them.

III.— Trailing Arbutus.

NED Brown has his pocket full of the flowers we were to bring today," said Allie, as we were ready to begin our lesson.

"O, Ned, you will smother the little things! Do bring them here."

"I don't believe they're what you want," said Ned bashfully, pulling out a handful of long vines with here and there a cluster of delicate little flowers.

"O, those are just what I meant!" answered the teacher. "And these are beautiful ones, too. Notice how fragrant they are! What made you think they were not the kind that I wanted, Ned?"

"I don't know, they *trail* and they have *fragrant pink clusters of flowers*, as you said. But I found them in such a sandy old place and the leaves are so coarse - I – I was afraid they weren't very good specimens, even if they were the right kind."

"O, Ned, Ned! If you could even learn to have just a little faith in yourself and in the things you do. Do you remember the hard problem you reasoned out so nicely last week and thought it must be wrong merely because it was you that reasoned it? Ned, you are one of the few boys that need to learn to have more respect for yourself. Now this piece of trailing arbutus — you could not have found a more beautiful, more perfect spray of it, had you searched the world over.

"As to the leaves that seemed to you so mean, you will always find them like this. Rather coarse, brown leaves, to be sure, but that is because they have been alive under the snow all winter. This plant is what is called an 'evergreen;' that is, a plant which, like the pine and the hemlock, keeps its foliage all winter. And as to the 'sandy, old place' in which you found them, that just is the very best kind of soil to find them in. They could not live in the heavy, rich soil of our gardens.

This flower is a sister to the huckleberry, the cranberry, the checkerberry. It has, too, some aristocratic sisters in the rhodora, the azalea, the laurel. All flower children belong to the

TRAILING ARBUTUS (*May Flower*).

HEATH FAMILY.

The Heaths are:

1. Monopetalous.

2. They are distinguished generally by the anthers opening by a little pore or hole at the top of each cell.

3. They have twice as many, or just as many stamens as petals.

Now let us examine this little flower.

Notice this pretty, tube-shaped corolla, divided at the top, so that at first glance one might almost think it polypetalous. Cut the corolla open, Ned, so that we prove that it is monopetalous.

And how nicely it fits into this little cup-shaped calyx! How plainly we can see the one pistil! And the *ten stamens*, with the little yellow anther on the top. And do you notice anything unusual about the stem?

"The stem is woolly or hairy; then, too, the inside of the corolla is covered with little fine hairs. I thought, since the plant lives through the winter, perhaps the woolly or hairy covering might be to help to keep it warm," said Harry, with a wise look.

"Who knows but that may be so?" answered the teacher. "Surely it is cold enough where it lives to need all the coverings it can get."

This is often called the "Mayflower." Indeed that name was given it by the Pilgrims who settled, you remember, in 1620, on the cold, barren coast of Massachusetts. During the cold, hard winter while they were building their houses and felling the great trees, these pilgrims suffered terribly from cold and hunger and homesickness. I'm inclined to believe, brave though they were, there were many times when they would have been glad enough to wake up some fine morning and find themselves comfortably situated in the warm houses of the country they had left.

But the winter passed away. The sun rose higher and higher, the days grew longer and longer, and the winds grew warmer and warmer. The snow was disappearing fast, and bits of green earth began to peep out here and there. By and by there sprang up all around the pine groves of old Plymouth a sweet little flower, pink and white, and so delicate and beautiful!

"O, let us call it the Mayflower — from the good old ship that brought us over!" said the Pilgrims. "Beautiful little flower, we never saw you on English soil! And you are so brave to peep out so early from the cold snow to give us welcome. Surely we will call you our Mayflower."

HEATH FAMILY.

MONOPETALOUS.
Anthers generally open by a hole at the top - As many or twice as many stamens as petals.

TRAILING ARBUTUS.
A trailing evergreen - Coarse, roundish leaves - Salver-shaped corolla - Corolla falls off after blossoming.

For our next lesson, I want the boys to put on their big rubber boots and get some beautiful *golden-yellow flowers* with *roundish, uncut leaves*. While the boys are wading about in damp places where these golden-yellow flowers are to be found, let the girls gather some little white nodding flowers with *very much cut leaves*. The flowers are coming so fast now we shall have to hurry along to keep pace with them."

DAFFY-DOWN-DILLY.

POOR little daffy-down-dilly!
    She slept with her head on a rose.
When a sly moth-miller kissed her,
    And left some dust on her nose.

Poor little daffy-down-dilly!
    She woke when the clock struck ten,
And hurried away to the fairy queen's ball,
    Down in the shadowy glen.

Poor little daffy-down-dilly!
    Right dainty was she, and fair,
In her bodice of yellow satin,
    And petticoat green and rare.

But to look in her dew-drop mirror,
    She quite forgot when she rose,
And into the queen's high presence
    Tripped with a spot on her nose.

Then the little knight who loved her —
    O, he wished that he were dead:
And the queen's maid began to titter,
    And tossed her saucy head.

And up from her throne so stately,
    The wee queen rose in her power,
Just waved her light wand o'er her,
    And she changed into a flower.

Poor little daffy-down-dilly!
    Now in silver springtime hours,
She wakes in the sunny meadows,
    And lives with other flowers.

Her beautiful yellow bodice,
    With green skirts wears she still,
And the children seek and love her,
    But they call her daffodil.

IV. - Marsh Marigold and Anemones.

"WHO has the *yellow* flowers, with *uncut leaves* and *found in swampy places?*"

"I think these may be the ones. These cowslips," said Ned, coming forward with a handful.

"O yes, these are the very flowers! But we must not call them cowslips. The real cowslip is very different. It is an English flower, very much smaller than this, and has groups of blossoms at the end of quite a tall stem. But the name for these is Marsh Marigold.

I remember telling our housemaid one day that she must call them by their right names. 'Pooh,' said she, 'cowslips is cowslips and nothin' else, and they is jest good for nothin' either, 'cept to bile for greens.' It's a good thing, children, to be practical and to have good common sense; but don't let us try to get beyond seeing the beautiful in every picture Mother Nature puts before us. I know one poor, ignorant, overworked woman who can never seem to see anything in a sunset, however beautiful, except an indication for a good wash-day on the morrow. Don't ever grow like that, girls; and, boys, don't ever grow like the man we read about in Longfellow a few days ago, who showed his coarse nature by snapping off the heads of the flowers with his cane as he passed along. In this work-a-day world of ours there

MARSH MARIGOLD.

is little danger of growing too fine in our appreciation of the beautiful.

But you will think I am preaching to you. I don't mean to do that; and I'm sure you'll forgive me this time, for the flowers are so beautiful and sweet, I think they really made me preach. But what do we find in these bright, golden flowers?

"I should have thought this plant belonged to the Crow-foot Family if the leaves had been different," said Harry, who was, as you see, one of those pupils who could remember and apply what his teacher had told him.

"I am glad you tried to place it in its family, Harry, even if you carried it miles away from its right home. It gives me courage always to see my boys and girls try. And you were right, Harry, this plant is a Crow-foot, although its leaves are not 'compound or much parted.' Perhaps you have heard the old saying that 'it is the exception that proves the truth of any rule.' This seems to be one of those exceptions; but, by and by, when you come to really analyze flowers with the 'reference table,' you will find this among the Crow-foots described as a flower with:

Pistils more than one-seeded - No petals. - Petal-like sepals, golden-yellow - Sepals not falling when the flower opens - Leaves rather rounded, not cut.

There is another flower in this same family — the Globe Flower, very much like the Marsh Marigold, whose leaves are deeply cut. That and the paler yellow of the blossom are the only distinguishing features between these two.

ANEMONE.

Among the country people in Old England, the Marsh Marigold is called the Horse Buttercup; and the Buttercup is looked upon as an 'insane herb,' that is, the smell of the flowers was supposed to produce insanity. A gentleman who has written a book on flower legends says that once when travelling through an English village he heard an old woman say to a little rosy-cheeked child, 'Joan, Joan, throw away those crazy flowers! Quick! Quick! Don't you know the smell of them will make you mad?'

"I am glad we have no such foolish fear of these beautiful yellow flowers now. Not to gather buttercups in the green fields in the springtime would indeed be a 'golden opportunity' lost.

"And now let us see the little white, nodding flowers with the much-cut leaves that the girls were to bring. Here they are! How pink some of them are! And here are some with a real purplish tinge!

These little flowers have such a pretty name, too. It is one of those soft, sweet-sounding words that one likes to say, -

And that reminds me, I saw in an old magazine a few days ago an odd little device for learning to pronounce this word. I'm sure, such puzzle-loving children as you are, you'll be glad to see it.

__________**M**________________________**E**

"What two capital letters have I printed, Allie?"
"An M and an E."
Now let me put the M on the E,

M
E

and we have our delicate little flower's name.

An M on E, or as it is spelled, *Anemone*.

"Now let us examine the flower. There are four kinds of Anemones, but this is, I think, the prettiest of them all. Notice how smooth it is in all its parts — the leaves, the stem, the flower. Notice the little whorl of stem-leaves — but they are not close up to the flower, deceiving us into half-believing them to be its calyx, as you remember they were in the Hepatica. These petals again are not petals at all, but are colored sepals, just as they were in the Hepatica and in the Marsh Marigold.

"A common name for the little Anemone is Wind Flower. It was given that name long ago by the simple country folk because, as an English couplet says, they noticed that it is a:

> "Coy flower, that ne'er uncloses her lips
> Until the wind doth on them blow."

There is also this story connected with the gentle little Anemone. There was once a golden-haired, bright-faced boy, Adonis, whom the beautiful Venus loved most tenderly. But the loves of these gods and goddesses seemed always to be fated. Something very sad was sure to happen, if we may believe the myths of those times. And so the beautiful Adonis, one day, while hunting, came to a most terrible death. Venus was inconsolable. Her beautiful boy, Adonis, dead! Throwing herself upon a bank in the

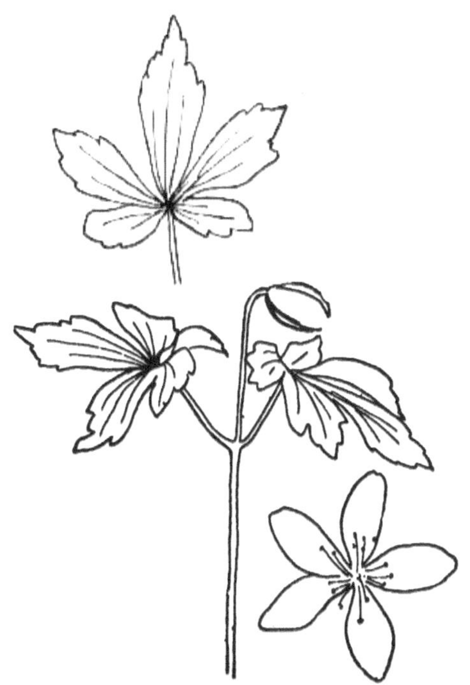

LEAVES AND FLOWER OF ANEMONE.

grove where the lad had been so cruelly slain, she wept bitter, bitter tears. But even her tears were immortal - and where they fell, there sprang up a delicate little white flower — the Anemone.

There is another flower connected in story with Venus and Adonis — a blood-red flower, called the Adonis flower, and supposed to have sprung from the blood-drops of the slain Adonis.

ANEMONE.

Flowers single on long stalks — No petals — Calyx of from 5 to 15 petal-like sepals — Upper leaves in whorls — Leaves much cut — Many pistils.

MARSH MARIGOLD

Leaves not cut — No petals — Golden-yellow sepals — One pistil.

THE MARIGOLD.

"Open afresh your round of starry folds,
Ye ardent marigolds!
Dry up the moisture of your golden lids,
For great Apollo bids
That in these days your praises shall be sung
On many harps, which he has lately strung;
And then again your dewiness he kisses—
Tell him I have you in my world of blisses
So haply when I rove in some far vale,
His mighty voice may come upon the gale."

—KEATS.

HOW AN APPLE TREE GROWS.

HEN a young seed begins to grow, it starts with one little cell. This cell is a kind of round bag, or tiny bladder. It is hollow, and has in it a sort of jelly. Those who study plants can, with their microscopes, watch just how the young seed grows. When first they observe the tiny sack, or cell, it is not larger than the point of a pin. They can see it grow larger, but even when it is full-grown it is no larger than the dot over this letter "i."

Next, they can see a very thin wall - thinner than the thinnest paper - growing inside of the little cell. This wall or partition grows quite across from one side to the other, making two little cells of it.

After this, a partition grows in each of these two cells, making four. And so the seed goes on growing, by each of the cells dividing into two or more.

All plants grow in this way. But each plant will grow according to its own seed. The seed of a turnip will begin to grow with one cell and then make cell after cell, with all the cells packed pretty close together. But all these cells will grow together in such a way as to make a turnip-plant. An acorn will grow in the same way; but all its cells will grow together in such a way as to make an oak tree.

Think of a large apple tree. First, it began with a tiny cell in the bottom of a pistil of an apple blossom. Out of this cell grew two other cells. Then out of them grew more cells. And so they kept on until the whole seed was ripe.

Now here is something very curious. All those little cells in that little apple seed grew in such a way that they actually made a little apple tree inside of that little seed. There they made a minute pair of leaves and a minute point of a root. When the tiny cells had their tiny plant completed, the seed was ripe.

The apple fell from the tree, the seed entered the ground, and in the spring the wet in the soil below and the heat from the sun above burst open the seed. Then out came the little point of a root, and, not liking the light, grew downwards into the ground.

But while the little point of a root was doing this, the little pair of leaves, folded up in the seed, also began to grow, and, loving the light, pushed their way up where they could feel the warm sunshine.

There the little pair of leaves spread out. Then up

between them grew the little stem. Then more leaves came out; and still, the stem kept pushing up, and still, more leaves kept coming.

Moreover, while the plant was growing above the ground, the little root underground was branching and growing larger, and with all its fine young hollow hairs was sucking up the water from the soil to go up to the leaves, which took in the air that some of it might mix with the sap to make the very stuff that forms the little cells.

The roots and leaves work together to build up the plant. The roots take water from the ground, but that alone would not make cells. The cells must have carbon, and this the plant obtains mostly from the air by breathing it through the leaves.

So whatever the plant may be — a great forest tree or a spear of grass — its cells are made of carbon and water. The whole tree is made of these cells — trunk, roots, branches, leaves, flowers, and fruit.

Look at a large oak tree. Can it be that that immense plant is made of nothing but a mass of tiny cells not larger than the dot of an "i" — and not so large? It can be. It is so.

FAWN-FOOTED NANNIE.

Fawn-footed Nannie, where have you been?
"Chasing the sunbeams into the glen,
Plunging thro' silver lakes after the moon,
Tracking o'er meadows the footsteps of June."

Fawn-footed Nannie, what did you see?
"Saw the fays sewing leaves on a tree;
Saw the waves counting the eyes of the stars,
Saw cloud-lamps sleeping by sunset's red bars."

Nannie, dear Nannie, take me with you,
So I may listen and see as you do.
"Nay; you must borrow my ear and my eye,
Or music will vanish and beauty will die."

V – Buttercup, Dandelion, Coltsfoot.

CROWFOOT OR LATE BUTTERCUP

"For today's lesson, we were to bring three flowers — all yellow, alike in color, but in everything else very unlike.

The Buttercup, of which we spoke last week incidentally, and with which you are all so familiar, is another of the Crowfoots."

"I thought of that the very minute I noticed the leaves!" cried Allie, speaking in her enthusiasm right out in school.

"Yes, indeed, these are genuine Crowfoot leaves if ever there were any. Notice how easily the petals fall. I hope we shall all be willing to sweep about our desks when we have finished our flower lesson; for it is a distinguishing characteristic of this flower that its petals fall early. In the botanies, a description of the Buttercup would hardly be completed if that were not mentioned.

"And at last, we have found a Crowfoot that has petals and sepals both. I feared you would begin to think all Crowfoots were petal-less. But this is a real, genuine Crowfoot — a typical Crowfoot in every respect.

"I am glad you brought in the Dandelions. They are such pretty sunny flowers. If they grew in our gardens and we had to work hard to keep them alive, I suppose we should value their gold as they deserve."

"But they are such funny flowers," said Harry with a puzzled air. "There seem to be pistils and stamens all over the blossom. Why, last night, I pulled off a petal and put it under my magnifying glass and it seemed as if I had a whole flower there."

"That is just what you did have, Harry. This is the first compound flower we have had. You know — at least you are trying to learn — what compound numbers are. Perhaps you remember the day when Allie, almost discour-

DANDELION.
a, plant; b, blossom; c, d, fuit.

aged over them, defined them as 'a lot of numbers joined together.' Now a compound flower is a lot of flowers joined together. Let us pull off a petal of the Dandelion, cut it open, and find within the pistil and stamens. You did not know, did you, that when you gather dandelion blossoms you gather just so many bouquets of flowers? The flowers have many a secret hidden away in their wise little heads that we never so much as dream of."

"This other yellow flower, the Coltsfoot, is a compound flower too. It is not as common as the dandelion. Let us all look at it through my large strong glass. Do you see there are two kinds of florets growing on the same head? The outer ones have pistils and no stamens; but the central ones have both pistils and stamens.

One odd thing about this plant is that its leaves do not come until its flowers are all gone. They are odd-looking leaves — heart-shaped with angles, soft and downy on the underside, growing on long, leaf stems as white and downy as they are themselves. This herb is supposed to be good for coughs; and, as you all know, I presume, there is a sort of cough candy made from it — at least it has the name of Coltsfoot given it.

> I love thee well, my dainty flower!
> My wee, white, cowering thing,
> That shrinketh like a cottage maid,
> Of bold, uncivil eyes afraid,
> Within thy leafy ring!"
>
> —MRS. SOUTHEY.

BUTTERCUP.

BELATED.

SINGLE buttercup I found,
    A star upon my weary way,
As summer closed her heated round,
    And ushered in the autumn day.

A little memory of May,
    That slept too late, as I have done,
And so unknowingly gone astray,
    And now stood lonely in the sun.

It seemed with anxious look to ask,
    Are all my bright companions dead?
Or have I slept, forgetting task,
    Until the lovely May has sped?

There waves around me autumn grain;
    I see the ripened apples shine:
I feel the patter of the rain;
    I see the grapes that blush with wine.

Ay, yes, I slept, I sweetly dreamed,
    Of babbling brook and azure sky,

And in my foolish fancy deemed
    That flowers like me would never die.

From such a dream why should I wake,
    Afar and in another zone —
Wake only that the heart may break
    To find myself alone, alone?

And this it is to live too long,
    To overpass our proper time,
And hear, instead of merry song,
    The bells of death in solemn chime.

So, too, with man; youth slept away,
    He wakes to find a useless age,
And wearily from day to day
    Drags out an aimless pilgrimage."

—WHITTIER.

There is a tongue in every leaf —
    A voice in every rill;
A voice that speaketh everywhere -
In flood and fire, through earth and air,
    A tongue that is never still.

—ANON.

THE TREE THAT TRIED TO GROW.

NE time there was a seed that wished to be a tree. It was fifty years ago, and more than fifty — a hundred perhaps.

But first there was a great bare granite rock in the midst of the Wendell woods. Little by little, dust from a squirrel's paw, as he sat upon it eating a nut, fallen leaves, crumbling and rotten, - and perhaps the decayed shell of a nut, - made earth enough in the hollows of the rock for some mosses to grow and for the tough little saxifrage flowers which seem to thrive on the poorest fare, and look all the healthier, like very poor children.

Then one by one, the mosses and blossoms withered and turned to dust; until after years and years and years, there was earth enough to make a bed for a little feathery birch seed which came flying along one day.

The sun shone softly through the forest trees; the summer rain pattered through the leaves upon it and the seed felt wide awake and full of life. So it sent a little pale-green stem up into the air, and a little white root down into the shallow bed of the earth. But you would have been surprised to see how much the root found to feed upon in only a handful of dirt.

Yes, indeed! And it sucked and sucked away with its little hungry mouths, till the pale-green stem became a small brown tree, and the roots grew tough and hard.

So, after a great many years, there stood a tall tree as big round as your body, growing right upon a large rock, with its big roots striking into the ground on all sides of the rock, like a queer sort of wooden cage.

Now, I do not believe there was ever a boy in this world who tried as hard to grow into a wise, or a rich, or a good man, as this birch seed did to grow into a tree, that did not become what he wished to be. And I don't think anybody who hears the story of the birch tree, growing in the woods of Wendell, need ever give up to any sort of difficulty in his way, and say, "I can't." Only try as hard as the tree did, and you can do everything.

—FRANCIS LEE.

WHEN THE APPLE BLOSSOMS STIR.

The buds in the tree's heart safely were folded away,
Awaiting in dreamy quiet the coming of May,

When one little bud roused gently and pondered awhile;
"It's dark, and no one would see me," it said with a smile.

"If I, before all the others, could bloom first in May,
And so be the only blossom, if but for a day,

How the world would welcome my coming, - the first little
    flower, -
'Twill surely be worth the trouble if but for an hour."

Close to the light it crept softly, and waited till Spring,
With her magic fingers, the door wide open should fling.

Spring came, the bud slipped out softly and opened its eyes
To catch the first loving welcome; but saw with surprise,

That swift through the open doorway, lo, others had burst!
For thousands of little white blossoms had thought to be first.

- ST. NICHOLAS. "JACK-IN-THE-PULPIT"

JUNE-BERRY.

VI. – Shad-blow or June-berry – Saxifrage.

AND now we come to another family. The Bloodroot, you remember, was a Poppy, the Trailing Arbutus was a Heath, and now this pretty branch of white blossoms from the Shad-blow or June-berry is - you'd hardly believe it, but it is - a Rose.

Let us read the description of the Rose Family.

Alternate leaves with stipules - Regular flowers; - their petals and stamens inserted on a persistent calyx; Few seeds.

This Rose Family is certainly as large a family as we

find among these flower people; perhaps because it is useful and beautiful as well. Its members are old friends of ours, many of them. There are the pretty dwarf Flowering Almond that we like so much to see in our gardens, the Peach, the Plum, the Cherry, the Apple, the Pear and the Quince trees - all belonging to the Rose Family. Indeed, I don't know what we should do without this family. Certainly fruit lovers would think life wasn't worth living without it.

And now, examining this bit of Shad-bush or June-berry, we find first the family traits - those we should always look for first. Here are two pistils - though there may be any number from two to five - and though the styles are separate, the seed-cradles are united. The petals are rather long and narrow. The fruit, if we had any here, we should find to be berry-like, having several cells with only one or two seeds in a cell.

Now, Jenny, if you will distribute the little white flowers you have, we will examine those. Such little flowers - and such neglected flowers too, I think. Not one person in a hundred knows how brave they are, or how beautiful. Where did you find them, Jenny?

"They were growing all along the road to school; but these I gathered out upon the ledge. They were growing in the little clefts and in the little hollow places on the top. It seemed as if some of them had no soil at all to grow from."

When you know that the name of the flower was given it for that very reason, that it seemed to grow out from the very rock, you will be glad you noticed how little soil it

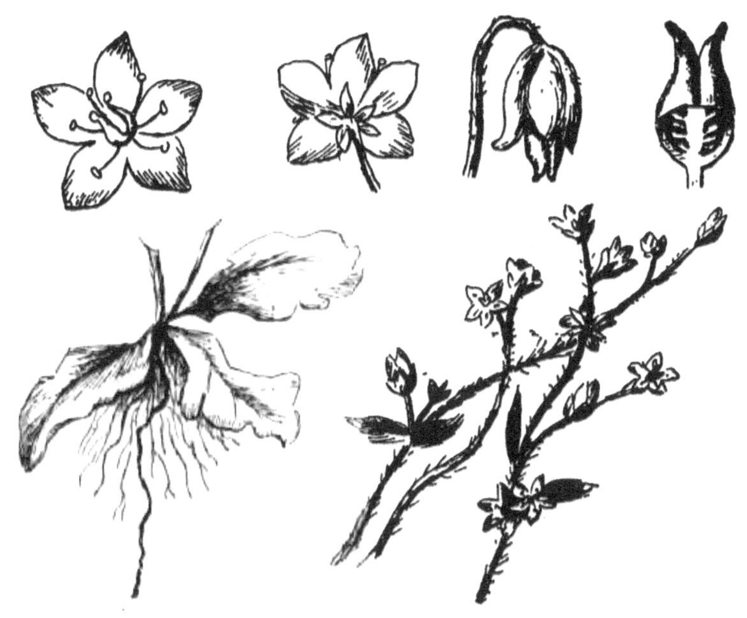

VIRGINIA SAXIFRAGE.

needed. Indeed, it does seem as if it had no soil. Therefore, someone gave it the name of Saxifrage, a word made up of two Latin words, *Saxem* meaning a rock and *frangere* meaning *to break*.

We can learn very little of this flower without the use of our strongest microscope. Here is a flower cut down through the middle ready to be examined.

Notice the little green calyx, the five-parted corolla growing upon the calyx; the ten stamens also inserted upon the calyx; the two pistils joined together in an ovary, which looks like a little chest with two compartments, each brimful of seeds.

The Saxifrage is the most common; but there are others. I have seen in a choice herbarium a bright yellow specimen of Saxifrage, and also a delicate purple one with bluish-green leaves up and down the stem. Another kind called Bishop's Cap grows eight or ten inches tall, has close-sitting leaves up and down the stem but leaves with foot-stalks at the base.

This little Saxifrage or stone-breaker was believed by the ancients to really break through rocks by some unknown power which was given it by the gods. You will be surprised perhaps to know, too, that the great flowering Hydrangea and the Syringa bush in our gardens are own sisters to this modest little Saxifrage.

ROSE FAMILY.

Alternate leaves with stipules - Regular flowers, their petals and stamens inserted on a persistent calyx - Few seeds.

SHADBUSH.

Rather long, narrow petals - Pistils two to five - Separate styles inserted in the ovary - Berry-like fruit, - several one or two-seeded cells.

SAXIFRAGE FAMILY.

Fewer pistils than petals more or less united - Four or five petals on the calyx - Stamens five or ten - Saxifrage (Virginiensis) - Leaves clustered at the root - Flowers on a scape in groups - White flowers - Early spring.

PAINTED TRILLIUM.

VII. – Trillium.

E'VE found some flowers today that look for all the world like the flowers we make in the squares and triangles of our drawing books, they are so exactly alike in every-thing. Willie says they are as "set" as an old Puritan.

Sure enough! You have found a Trillium; and I'm sure you will all agree it is well named, for indeed it is tri-leaved, tri-petaled, tri-celled, tri-everything.

This one is a Painted Trillium, the prettiest of them all, I think. If Mother Nature ever does "conventionalize" any of her flowers as we do in our drawing books, I think she does it in this flower, and she does it well.

There are six kinds of Trillium - the Nodding, the Erect, the Recurved, the Great-flowered, and the Painted Trillium. The last has very delicate pink-purple lines at the base of its petals, supposed to be the work of the fairies. These Trilliums and the Indian Cucumber-root, which perhaps you will find by and by, are the only members of the Trillium Family known in our country.

TRILLIUM FAMILY.

Herbs - Simple stems rising from a short root-stalk - Leaves in a whorl - Perfect, very regular flowers.

NODDING TRILLIUM.

Leaves nearly close-sitting - Small flowers whose flower stalk curves down under the leaves - Recurved, wavy, pointed petals.

TO A MOUNTAIN DAISY, ON TURNING IT DOWN WITH A PLOUGH.

WEE, modest, crimson-tipped flower,
 Thou's met me in an evil hour;
For I maun crush amang the stoure[1]
 Thy slender stem;
To spare thee now is past my power,
 Thou bonnie gem!

 Alas! It's no' thy neebor sweet,
The bonnie lark, companion meet!
Bending thee 'mang the dewy weet,[2]
 Wi' speckled breast,

When upward springing, blithe, to greet
 The purpling east.

1 Dust.
2 Rain Wetness.

Cauld blew the bitter, biting north
Upon thy early, humble birth;
Yet cheerfully thou glinted[3] forth,
        Amid the storm!
Scarce reared above the parent earth
        Thy tender form.

The flaunting flowers our gardens yield,
High sheltering woods and wa's[4] maun shield
But thou, beneath the random bield[5]
        O' clod or stane.
Adorns the histie[6] stibble field,
        Unseen, alane.

There, in thy scanty mantle clad,
Thy snawie bosom sunward spread,
Thou lifts thy unassuming head
        In humble guise;
But now the share uptears thy bed,
And low thou lies!

Such is the fate of simple bard,
On life's rough ocean luckless starr'd!
Unskillful he to note the card
        Of prudent lore,
Till billows rage, and gales blow hard,
        And whelm him o'er.

Such fate to suffering worth is given.
Who long with wants and woes has striven, -
By human pride or cunning driven
        To misery's brink,
Till wrench'd of every stay but Heaven,
        He, ruined, sink.

3   Peeped.
4   Walls.
5   Shelter.
6   Dry.

E'en thou who mourn'st the daisy's fate,
That fate is thine, - no distant date,
Stern ruin's plowshare drives, elate,
    Full on thy bloom;
Till crush'd beneath the furrow's weight,
    Shall be thy doom!

- ROBERT BURNS.

VIII. – Adder's Tongue, or Dog-tooth Violet, and Bellwort or Wild Oat.

ERTAINLY if there was ever any truth in the "Doctrine of Signatures" this plant would have been the grand panacea for snake-bites for never was there a more snake-like leaf than this. No wonder people came to call it Adder's Tongue!

How much it looks like a lily! Indeed it does belong to the Lily Family and not to the Violet Family as you might perhaps think it ought, judging from its other common name of Dog-tooth Violet.

There is the bell-shaped corolla that always reminds us of a lily. Notice that it has six petals and six stamens. A noticeable feature of this flower is the six-sided stigma. There seems to be hardly any style, it is so short. These, together with its spotted leaves and its scape, is description enough, I think, to distinguish it from any other plant.

You have here another little bell-shaped flower. It always seemed to me these two flowers are enough alike to be first-cousins at least.

Indeed, the Colchicum Family, to which this other little bell-like flower belongs, and the Lily Family, to which the Dog-tooth Violet belongs, do have certain traits in common. For example, both are parallel-veined; both have perfect flowers; the perianth is usually of six parts, and the ovary in both is three-celled. In other respects, however, there is a difference; for example, in this other little flower - the Bellwort or Wild Oat, as some call it, we have sessile leaves, while in the Dog-tooth Violet we have a scape; the leaves in the Wild Oat are plain; in the Dog-tooth Violet they are spotted; in the Wild Oat the three styles are more or less separate; in the Dog-tooth Violet, there is the one style or at least there are three styles united so as to look like one, the stigmas even being united.

LILY FAMILY.

Parallel-veined leaves - Perfect regular flowers - Perianth six parted - Stamens as many as petals - Anthers turn inward - One pistil - One style - Three celled ovary - Fruit a pod or berry.

DOG-TOOTH VIOLET OR ADDER'S TONGUE.

Two leaves - spotted - Scale - roundish - ovary - Long Style - club-shaped - Erect anthers - Stigmas united - Bell-shaped perianth.

COLCHICUM FAMILY.

Parallel-veined leaves - Perfect, regular flowers - Perianth six-parted - Stamens as many as petals - Anthers turn outward - Three styles - Three-celled ovary.

BELLWORT OR WILD OAT.

Sessile leaves - plain - Styles united at their base - Bell-shaped perianth.

THE WATER LILY.

In a brook which loved to stray
O'er yellow sand and pebble gray
The lily of the silvery hue
All fleshy dwelt, with white leaves wet,
Away the sparkling water played,
Through bending grass and fragrant flowers;
Light and delight seemed all its dower;
Pale lovely splendor to the shade.

- J. H. REYNOLDS.

CATKIN OF WILLOW.

THE WILLOW AND THE BEE.

"GOOD afternoon, Mrs. Willow," said a bee to the big willow tree down by the brook, one day late in the fall.

"Good afternoon, Mrs. Bee," replied Mrs. Willow. "How do you do this beautiful, sun-shiny day? You look as if you had been flying a long way. Won't you come and rest yourself for a little while on one of my twigs?"

"Thank you, I will, Mrs. Willow, for to tell you the truth, I am just about tired out. You see, the queen bee has been making us work so hard lately to get all our cells filled with honey, that we working bees have been too busy to stop a minute. We're all through now, though, and she told us we could play today, as we might not have another chance for a good while.

"I didn't know what she meant, for I'm a new bee - I only came out of my egg last spring - so I asked a drone what was going to happen.

"He told me that soon Jack Frost would come and bring the winter. Then we could not fly over the fields anymore, but would have to stay in the hive till he went away, which would not be for a long, long time.

"O dear! I don't like it at all. I wish I were a willow tree, so I shouldn't have to be shut up.

"You have a pretty easy time, don't you, Mrs. Willow, with nothing to do all summer but let your leaves dance in the breezes?"

"Nothing to do! indeed, Mrs. Bee!" exclaimed the willow tree. "Do you think a mother with as many children as I have can be very lazy?"

"Children!" cried the bee; "I didn't know you had any children!"

"That's because you're so young; but I have, - thousands of them all over this tree. There's a baby now right under you." The bee jumped.

"Under me! Why, I don't see anything."

Then looking up closer he added, "There's nothing here but a little, hard, brown lump. That doesn't seem much like a baby!"

"Perhaps not, Mrs. Bee," replied Mamma Willow; "but if you could look inside, you'd find one fast asleep, wrapped in fur from head to toe."

"Every day this summer, when you thought me playing, I was busy getting these fur coats ready for my wee ones. They are so cozy and warm now, in their snug little cradles, that they'll sleep soundly until spring comes."

"Well, that's very strange, Mrs. Willow. I didn't know you had so much to do. And will the babies stay there all winter?"

"Yes, to be sure they will, and be as quiet as little mice. You shouldn't think that you bees are the only ones who sleep during the cold weather. I, too, must have rest, and now that the babies are taken care of, I'm ready to stop working.

"My, how chilly it is! Don't you think so, Mrs. Bee? Why, there's old Northwind! I wondered what made me so sleepy. Now that he's come, I shouldn't be one bit surprised if Jack Frost were here this very night! You'll be wise to fly home before you get cold, my little neighbor!"

"Yes, I think I ought to go; I didn't know it was so late. Good night, Mrs. Willow! Sweet dreams to you and the babies!"

"Good night, Mrs. Bee! Don't forget to come and see us all in the springtime!"

"I'll remember," answered the bee; and away she flew to her hive in the garden.

Mrs. Willow was right, for Jack Frost did arrive in a very short time.

When Florence and Fred awoke the next morning, they jumped up and down with delight at finding the ground covered with its fairy snowflakes. They knew what it meant much better than the robins, for Jack Frost was an old friend of theirs.

When they went out coasting, they would often go and

listen at the hive for the humming of the bees, but not a sound could be heard. Fred was afraid the bees were all dead, but Florence told him how they were taking their long winter nap, and she said that by and by they would come out and be as lively as ever.

It had been growing warmer for several days until, at last, one Saturday morning early in the spring, the sun's beams shone out so brightly that Jack Frost had to hurry back to Northland.

The children begged mamma to let them put on their rubber boots and go down into the meadow to see if the "pussies" had come out.

"We must go for Mary first," they said, after mamma had given her consent. "Then for a good time!"

"I see one pussy peeking out!" cried Fred as the three children stood under the willow tree. "There's another, Mary! And another! And another! Oh! How many! Please, Florence, hold me up on this stone so I can reach them!"

"We'll get a big bunch and send it to Charley Morrison, won't we? For he says they don't have pussy willows in the city."

"Pussy Willows!" buzzed a bee to herself as she flew around the tree. "Well, I didn't suppose anything really would come out of those little hard things. So that's what they call Willow's babies! Pussy Willows!"

PUSSY WILLOW

The brook is brimmed with melting snow,
    The maple sap is running,
And on the highest elm a crow
    His black wings is sunning.
A close green bud the Mayflower lies
    Upon its mossy pillow;
And sweet and low the south-wind blows,
And through the brown fields calling goes,
    "Come, Pussy! Pussy Willow!"
Within your close brown wrapper stir
Come out and show your silver fur
    "Come, Pussy! Pussy Willow!"
Soon red with bud the maple-trees,
    The bluebirds will be singing,
And yellow tassels in the breeze
    Be from the poplars swinging;
And rosy will the Mayflower lie
    Upon its mossy pillow;
But you must come the first of all, -
"Come, Pussy!" is the south wind's call, -
    "Come, Pussy! Pussy Willow!"
A fairy gift to children dear,
The downy firstling of the year, -
    "Come, Pussy! Pussy Willow!"

-COLUMBINE

COLUMBINES.

IX. - Columbine.

AND now at last we have the Columbine. I am so glad you brought it. It is such an odd flower, so pretty, and so richly colored.

It doesn't look much like the delicate little Anemone and Hepatica, does it? And still, it is an own sister; but then you know there is quite apt, in a large humble family, to be some one member who seems to make up in style and elegance for all the rest. Perhaps it is so among flower-people as well. You remember we found the modest little Bloodroot to be an own sister to the bright red Poppy, and the little common Saxifrage could claim kinship with the haughty garden Hydrangea.

Now for a sharp examination of the new member of our

COLUMBINE

old Crowfoot Family. See the five sepals that look for all the world like petals; then notice the odd, tube-shaped petals themselves, drawn out into this long, spurred honey-cell. I dare say you all know how sweet tasting these horns of the Columbine are. There seem to be many stamens; but the pistils - just five - you can easily count. The seed-vessel of the plant is strange enough - a kind of pod which has openings up and down its sides. And its Latin name is *Aquilegia* from the word *Aquila* meaning eagle.

The early botanists seem to have been as imaginative regarding the flowers as the early Greeks were regarding the stars. You remember not long since we read the story of a group of stars, which were named Aquila from some fancied resemblance to an eagle.

The star group is connected with one of the stories of the seven sisters, or the Pleiades.

THE SEVEN SISTERS

These seven sisters were very devoted and were always together. Orion, the hunter, pursued them through the wood, over hill and dale. Notwithstanding their fleet-footedness, Orion had nearly overtaken them, when Jupiter caught them up and placed them together in the sky far from the reach of harm. There are only six of them to be seen, but that does not spoil the story at all, for it is said that at one time, when there was a terrible battle going on down on the earth, one of the sisters hid herself in terror behind the others. One would suppose that she would have come out after the battle was over, but it seems she never has. Another story accounting for her absence is that she fell in love with a mortal and gave up her place in the heavens to come down and dwell with him. Since it is all a myth, you can take your choice of the stories; but for the sake of our eagle story we must this time accept the last version; for then I can tell you that when this sister came to die, Juno, not willing that she should be lost, changed her into a beautiful strong eagle. The sister, grateful to the kind goddess, soared proudly up into the air, higher and higher up above the clouds, away into the blue sky, and took her place with outstretched wings among the everlasting constellations.

COLUMBINE

Five petals spur-shaped - Five sepals - Pistils two to five, and separate - Ovary more than one-seeded - Pods in fruit.

DISCONTENT

DOWN in a field, one day in June,
    The flowers all bloomed together,
Save one who tried to hide herself,
    And drooped, that pleasant weather.

A robin who had flown too high,
    And felt a little lazy,
Was resting near this buttercup,
    Who wished she were a daisy.

For daisies grow so trim and tall!
    She always had a passion
For wearing frills around her neck,
    In just the daisies' fashion.

And buttercups must always be

The same old tiresome color;
While daisies dress in gold and white,
    Although their gold is duller.

"Dear robin," said this sad young flower,
    "Perhaps you'd not mind trying
To find a nice white frill for me,
    Some day when you are flying?"

"You silly thing!" the robin said,
    "I think you must be crazy
I'd rather be my honest self
    Than any made-up daisy.

You're nicer in your own bright gown;
    The little children love you;
Be the best buttercup you can,
    And think no flower above you.

Though swallows leave me out of sight,
    We'd better keep our places:
Perhaps the world would all go wrong
    With one too many daisies.

Look bravely up into the sky.
    And be content with knowing
That God wished for a buttercup
    Just here, where you are growing.

- SARA O. JEWETT.

OUR LAST FLOWER LESSON

AT the close of the lesson on the Columbine, our teacher had said, "The flowers are gaining upon us so fast, and the close of the term is so near at hand, perhaps it would be as well for us each to bring, if possible, a different flower for our next lesson. We can hardly more than have an introduction to them, perhaps only learn their names: still, that is better than nothing, for the flowers are such constant little friends and are so sure to all come again, we can at some other time cement our friendship with them by further acquaintance."

And such loads of flowers as we did bring! We had no idea there were so many kinds. A botany lesson every day through the whole summer would never have been enough for them all.

"It looks, children, as if we have work enough for a whole afternoon," said the teacher as she looked around the room. "It is like exhibition day with all these flowers! Let us begin work at once. Allie, distribute those little yellow flowers you have first. Such bright-faced little things as these are! Notice how regular they are - five little petals! And the leaves, alternate with stipules, look somewhat like strawberry leaves. The flower is flat and

CINQUE-FOIL

open; it has many stamens and many pistils. Do you see that the pistils are arranged in a little head? It belongs to the Rose family and its name is Cinque-foil, from the French for 'five-leaved' just as the Clover is called Tre-foil, meaning 'three-leaved.'"

And Harry has an odd-looking flower indeed! One almost wonders if it is a flower at all. Just see this pistil! If I take away the petals, it looks for all the world like an umbrella. And the leaves! Did ever a plant have such leaves as these! Is it any wonder, judging from them, that this plant is called the "pitcher plant" and the leaves monkey pitchers? They are bog-plants; and though I do not find much in this pitcher I have in my hand, but dirt and muddy

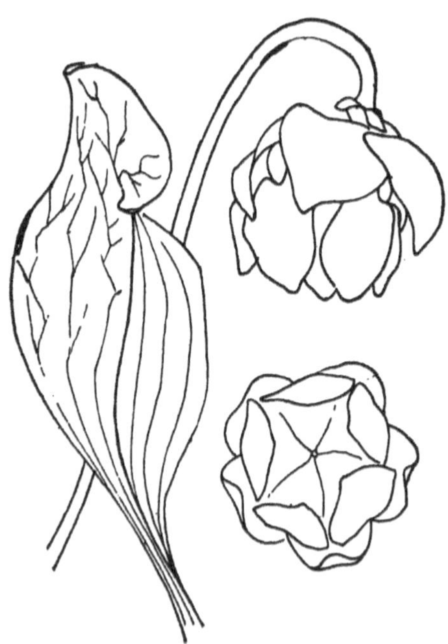

PITCHER PLANT.

water and dead insects, I have heard that in certain eastern countries there are pitcher plants with leaves so clean and large, that travelers are glad enough sometimes to drink from them. I once read of a traveler who had lost his way and was nearly perishing of thirst, when happily he came upon one of these pitcher plants. Whether this is true or not, I do not know; but I have often seen thirsty birds dipping their bills into these pitchers.

And here are Allie's flowers. Little delicate blue flowers! It was like you, Allie, to gather these. They take their name from their color and are called Bluets. I remember the first time I analyzed them, I carelessly called them polypetalous - judging from the four little lobes of the corolla. But if you split down the calyx you will find that they are monopetalous - a long tube-shaped corolla scalloped at its margin.

And Fred has a wonderful plant - a wise plant, indeed,

BLUETS. – *(Innocents.)*

for it can tell its own age. I am glad Fred was wise enough to dig down for its root, for the root is the part that is wise. Let me see - one, two, three - this plant is three years old. Four years old. How do I know? How does it tell me? Does anyone know?

"By the length of the root!"

"By the size of it!"

"By the color of it!"

"O, but I'm afraid you are merely guessing at it! Look sharply and examine closely."

"I see! the three-year-old root has three of those round places on it - the four-year-old has four.

"Yes, that is it; and those little round places are where from year to year a shoot has been sent up through the ground. Somebody fancied that these round places looked like seals, - kings' seals - so the name Solomon's Seal was

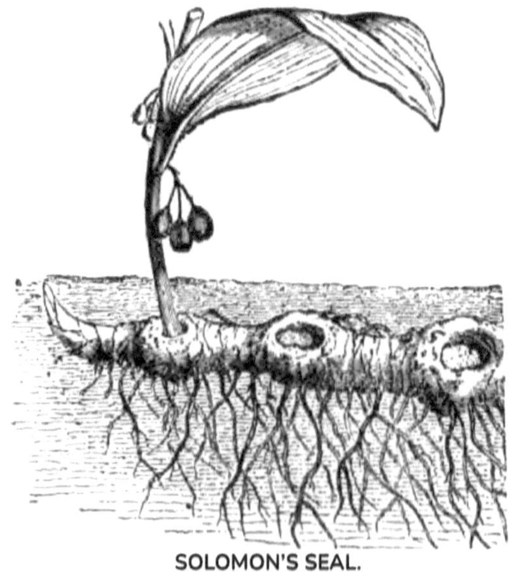

SOLOMON'S SEAL.

118

IRIS.

given to the plant. Solomon was very wise, you know; and certainly a plant that can tell its own age must be very wise also, I suppose."

And here is the pretty, wild Iris. I am glad you brought this, Walter. Did you ever see anything so oddly put together as this is? Certainly, this belongs to no "regular-flowered" family. Notice these stigmas! Even they look like petals. The color of this flower is very rich, and there is a pretty little legend told of it.

Read it, Allie, from this book:

LEGEND OF THE IRIS

The flowers, one day, assembled to celebrate a festival of the Rainbow. All came clothed in their wondrous beauty. But amidst them all, the beautiful blue Iris shone forth the loveliest. No other wore her rich robes and her sparkling jewels so gracefully. Her robe was deep blue like the twilight sky; and it was as softly shaded as the cloudlets.

Who could this fair stranger be! No one knew. 'Twas strange; but no one could name the fair flower so bright and so blue.

At last, some sister flower cried, "See, see! the rainbow colors of her beautiful robe!"

Just then the rain began to fall, the rainbow came out in all its glory, and sure enough there were the rainbow colors shining in the rain.

"Iris! Iris! The rainbow messenger!" cried the sister-flower. "Let us call her Iris!"

And Florence has an Orchid!

"Mother thought it was a Lady's Slipper," answered Florence, puzzled at the new word.

Yes, dear, a Lady's Slipper - belonging to the Orchid Family. These orchids are such queer flowers! I remember a teacher I once had in Botany used to say that when we found any strange, irregular flowers that looked like nothing under the sun, we might safely suspect it to be an orchid. These orchids have thick roots, the leaves are entire with parallel veins. The blossoms, no matter how

LADY'S SLIPPERS.

irregular they are, are always made up of six pieces - three outer and three inner – all colored. The lowest one is usually very large and is called "the lip".

LITTLE GIRL'S ADVICE TO CROCUS.

Miss Crocus, I know if I were you,
    I would not wake in the cold;
You shiver so when bleak winds blow,
    Shaking your bells of gold.

Now just keep down in your beds so brown,
    Till Spring is really here,
And bees shall come with merry hum,
    And frost you need not fear.

For I am sad when I should be glad,
    To see you all in a row, -
Purple, and white, and yellow bright,
    You sweetest flowers I know.

Since cold, cold rain will come again,
    Beating your tender heads,
Since Spring is late, please, Crocus, wait,
Snug in your little bed.

Then if you're wise you'll ope your eyes,
    When bluebirds come to sing;
When grass, you know, begins to grow,
    Then comes the *really* Spring.

ARETHUSA.

"I should think my flower might be an Orchid then," said Harry, holding up a beautiful purple blossom.

Yes, indeed, that is an Orchid - the Arethusa. How fragrant it is! It was named after Arethusa, a beautiful nymph who was changed by the goddess Diana into a fountain.

"Kittie has a queer-looking flower, too. It looks irregular enough to be an Orchid, I am sure," said Allie.

Yes, it does; but I wonder if it agrees with the description I gave you of an Orchid.

"I think not. It is irregular to be sure; but the calyx has five parts, there are only three petals. I found it under the Rhodora bush; and at first I thought it was the fallen petals of the Rhodora."

Your flower is a Polygala, Kittie. And an odd little flower it is, too! One singular thing about the Polygala is that most of them have, *under the ground*, another kind of flower. Dig some of these roots; you will be amused to find attached to them little sprays of greenish flowers.

And Harry has a bunch of Kalmia. If I should tell you that the Laurel has "pouch-like" petals, that alone would distinguish it from all other blossoms. A wheel-shaped flower, five-lobed, with ten pouches. There is the description of the Kalmia or American Laurel. There is another Laurel, a native of Southern Europe, called the "classic laurel," because so many poets have written about it.

It is a beautiful evergreen, with fragrant leaves, flowers, and berries, and often called Daphne, from a Grecian nymph of that name. You may like to hear the story connected with this laurel, though it is only a heathen myth or fable.

A long time ago, a charming nymph by the name of Daphne was beloved by the god Apollo; but by some of his rivals, she was transformed into a tree, which bore her name. Her lover, in despair, bound its leaves upon his temples, and from that hour the Daphne was sacred to Apollo. Now as Apollo was regarded as the patron and father of *poetry*, the "god of the golden lyre," branches of

KALMIA.

the sacred tree were afterward used to crown poets who attained great excellence. His temples were everywhere surrounded with these trees, and the priests and priestesses wore garlands of the fragrant leaves. An ancient Grecian festival, celebrated every ninth year in honor of Apollo, was called *Daphnephoria*, because all who took part in it bore branches of Daphne in the procession. It was a grand festival, the origin of which you will learn in Grecian history. I would tell it to you now, but I am afraid we shall have to leave many of our flowers unnamed. Time does fly so fast when scholars are busy!

Just one flower more, and we must leave our study of Botany till after vacation.

Chessie, bring me that odd-looking flower you have. I hardly need to tell you its name. All children know this is the "Jack-in-the-pulpit."

It belongs to the Arum Family, six members of which there are in all. They are all rather thick-set, fleshy people, rather sharp and acrid in their tastes. They have some very disagreeable traits that make them not very much of favorites in polite society.

For example, there is the Skunk Cabbage, that starts up in the early spring as a very pretty little purple spadix; but by and by, as it grows older, it spreads out some great coarse leaves and has such an unpleasant odor.

But this "Indian Turnip," or, as you children call it, the "Jack-in-the-Pulpit," has a spadix with such an odd little hood which it pulls over its head. The spadix looks for all the world as if it had fallen into the flower head-first. There are the blossoms down in the bottom of the cup, and the

JACK-IN-THE-PULPIT.

GALLA.

ARROW-ARUM.

other flowerless end is sticking up in full view under the hood. The Spadix is what you call Jack; and he does look indeed like the "priest all shaven and shorn." The sheath is his pulpit, and as he preaches in such large places and to such scattered audiences, I suppose the part that hangs over his head may act as a sort of "sounding-board," such as one sees sometimes in very old churches.

Beside the *Indian Turnip* and the *Skunk Cabbage*, there are the *Arrow-Arum*, whose spathe covers the entire length of the spadix, and whose leaves are arrow or heart-shaped; the *Calla*; the *Golden-Club*, which has no spathe; the *Green Dragon*, which has in fruit a cluster of red or deep orange berries; and last, but not least, as you boys will say, the "*Sweet-Flag.*"

In May, when sea-winds pierced our solitudes,
    I found the fresh Rhodora in the woods;
Spreading its leafless blooms in a damp nook,
To please the desert and the sluggish brook.
The purple petals, fallen in the pool,
    Made the black water with their beauty gay;
Here might the red-breast come, his plumes to cool,
    And court the flower that cheapens his array.

-EMERSON.

JACK-IN-THE-PULPIT.

Jack-in-the-pulpit is preaching today;
That's what the birds and the children say,
Preaching a sermon for them, you see,
Not heard by old folks, like you and me.

The birds trill his text o'er, "Spring-time is here,"
And the children quick echo, "Oh! Dear, Oh! Dear!"
Jack talks of tops and marbles and hoops,
Balls and bats, with no hint of books.

For out in the woods Jack holds church,
And who wants lessons with the smell of birch,
And odors of violets and all things sweet,
And birds with a chorus of "Tweet! Tweet?"

Haven't you seen them, the boys and girls
With laughing eyes and hair all curls,
Running to hear Jack's sermon, they say,
For them and the birds, this sweet spring day.

- ELLEN LEGARDE.

And now we must drop our study of Botany for a time. Keep your eyes open through the long vacation, gather the flowers that come, press them, and let us see them when the autumn term begins. Let us close our last lesson by reciting together the verse we have learned from Tennyson:

"Flower in the crannied wall,
I pluck you out of the cranny.
Hold you here, root and all, in my hand.
Little flower,- but if I could understand
What you are, root and all, and all in all,
I should understand what God and man is."

WATER-LILIES.

EXHIBITION DAY.

LTHOUGH our "Botany Lessons" were closed "for the season," there was one more good time ahead for us with our flower friends. On the morning of our Exhibition Day, we were to bring to the schoolhouse flowers and vines and leaves to decorate our hall with.

Never had we gathered our flowers with such zeal and interest. We shouted with delight over the flowers we knew, and we wondered and puzzled over those we did not know. Not a flower large or small, showy or modest but was inspected and commented on by "we wise ones," as Harry called us.

And when at just nine o'clock we were at the school building with our precious loads of flowers, how could we arrange and assort them without asking questions upon questions about them?

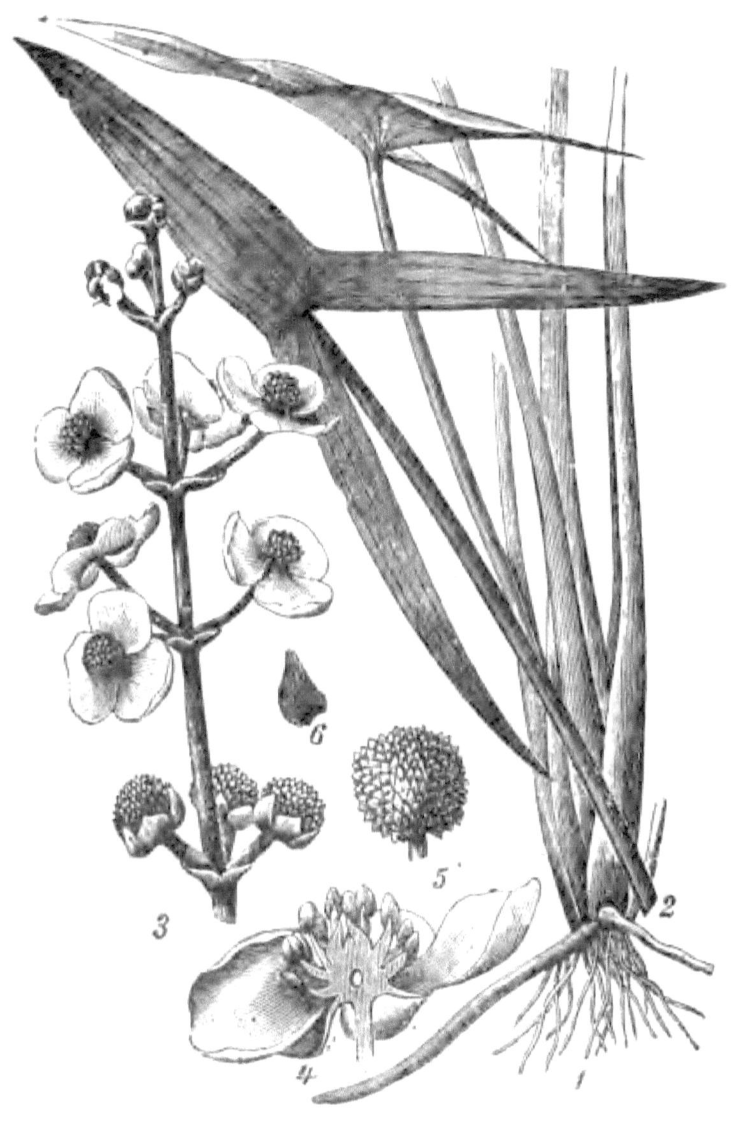

ARROW HEAD.

1, root; 2, stems and leaf; 3, flowers; 4, section of flower; 5. Fruit.

"We shall never get the hall ready," said our teacher, "if we do so much talking and so little work. Come, boys, festoon this clematis about the windows. It is a crowfoot as you might well suspect if you notice its ragged leaves, and its many stamens, its lack of any corolla, its white sepals, its leaves in threes, its creeping stem, its large, loose clusters of axillary flowers all tell us this is the clematis. And by and by, later in the season, you will find that its little seeds have long, feathery tails, making these present bunches of flowers look like bunches of fuzz."

Now let us arrange these Water Lilies and Sagittarias in these flat pans. They grow together in the water, why not keep them together here; they will look more natural and I'm sure they'll feel much more at home among all these other flower people if we have a little respect for their natural habitat in our arrangement of them. It always gives me "the creeps," as Margie calls it, to see land and water flowers, garden and wild flowers all mixed together. There is a certain "eternal fitness" of things that good taste, it seems to me, is bound to respect. Some people, you know, think it is beautiful to arrange seashells up and down the sides of their concrete walks, but it doesn't seem right. Emerson says, "Leave the seashells and the pebbles by the sea; they belong there - not in our parlors; and Emerson always knows 'what's what.'"

> "And to know
>   what's what is as high,
> As metaphysical wit may fly."

"Is this Sagittaria what we call Arrow-head?" asked Harry.

"Yes, and you can see for yourself why it is so called. Was there ever anything more like arrows than these leaves? All look sharply and see if you find anything peculiar in these flowers."

"The flowers grow in whorls of threes with leafy bracts at the base. Is that peculiar?"

"Well, hardly *peculiar*. It is a feature of the plant, though not a *peculiarity*."

"O, I see, I see!" cried Allie; "the flowers have three small green sepals, three large white petals, ever so many stamens - and - and but they are not all alike. The upper whorl has many stamens and no pistils, the lower whorl has a whole bunch of little ovaries crowded together in a little ball - a head, I suppose we should call it."

"That is just it, Allie; now here are two hard words for you to learn. Listen! when a plant has all the pistils in some flowers and all the stamens in others, such plants are called

MON OE CI OUS.

Sometimes all the pistils will be in flowers of one plant while all the stamens are in the flowers of another plant. Then such plants are called

DI OE CI OUS.

"How fragrant these water lilies are! Isn't it wonderful, children, that roots imbedded in the mud and slime of a pond can send up flowers of such sweetness and purity?"

"And here are some lotus blossoms! We read in our geography last week, you remember, of the Egyptian Lotus which, when the waters of the Nile sink back into their river bed, covers all the canals and pools of the country

LOTUS.

with its broad leaves and cup-shaped flowers. One kind of Lotus was considered a sacred flower by the Egyptians. It was dedicated to the Sun-god and was looked upon as an emblem of the *creation of the world from water*. That is why, in pictures of Egyptian art, we always see the Lotus blossom standing up so grandly, attracting as much, if not more, attention than the people and animals of the picture."

There was another kind of Lotus which was believed by these early people to have some very wonderful properties. The seed had a flavor very like ripe dates, and it was said to be a sovereign cure for homesickness and to have the marvelous power of making strangers who ate them forget their native country, their friends, and their family. Allie, get the little blue book on the shelf and read us what Ulysses has to say of the Lotus-Eaters. It will be just the story to listen to while we twist these evergreens into wreaths and garlands.

THE LOTUS-EATERS.

"You must know, O King (began Ulysses), that from the moment that I left the walls of Troy, victorious, the gods have been against me. At the very outset of my homeward voyage, great Neptune sent a storm upon me, by which I and my fleet were driven hither and thither by unfriendly winds quite out of our course, till at last we drifted to the strange island of the Lotus-Eaters. Here we landed, and I sent forward three of our men to find out what manner of men these Lotus-Eaters might be, while those who remained behind refilled our water-cruses and prepared a hasty banquet on the shore.

We waited and waited, but never a man of the three returned. At last, when we could no longer endure the suspense, we followed them, full of anxiety to learn their fate. What was our surprise to find them reclining at ease among the people of the land, on the flowery banks, under the pleasing shade of the lotus-tree.

The people seemed very kind and hospitable and welcomed us as they had welcomed our three companions.

'We have nothing to offer you,' they said, 'but the delicious fruit of the lotus-tree. But the lotus fruit is both meat and drink to us. We do not need to till the land nor tend the herds. The gods send us this fruit from the ever-fruitful trees, and here we sit eating and drinking through all the happy days.'

I was just about to taste the delicious-looking fruit when my eyes fell upon the three men whom we had sent forward to spy out the land.

Some strange change seemed to have passed over their faces. When I spoke to them, they looked at me with wild, bright eyes and answered me in a sort of far-off voice, like those who dream.

'Oh, let us alone!' they said - 'let us alone! Why have you come here to disturb us? Eat the fair fruit and drink its divine juices yourselves, but let us remain in peace in the flowery Lotus land!'

But I instantly commanded my companions, on pain of death, not to put that evil fruit to their lips. Then I urged the three men, by the memory of their homes in fair Ithaca, by the love they bore to their children and wives, to rise at once from the deathful feast and follow me.

But the Lotus-Eaters laughed a laugh of scorn. 'Know ye not, O strangers,' they said, 'that whoso tastes of our pleasant fruit shall never see wife nor children more? Return to your homes, ye who have not tasted, but let your three companions abide with us. It is not in their power to follow you, and they have lost even the wish to do so!'

But, with that, I signaled to my mates that they should seize the three dreamers and drag them away by main force back to the ship.

My mates hesitated for a moment, casting longing glances at the forbidden fruit; but either overawed by me or scared by the wild look of the dreamers, they laid hold on them and dragged their unwilling feet, with such haste as they might, back to the royal bark.

Then I commanded that if the three men offered any further resistance, they should be bound hand and foot under the benches of the many-benched ship.

But no sooner had the feet of the dreamers touched their own vessel than the spell was broken, and they awoke with glad hearts to take their place at the oars.

And we rowed hard all day, and at night we anchored in the peaceful harbor of Lach. Here, for some days, we cast anchor and feasted on the sports of our chase, and no man heeded or hindered us.

But when the third morning glittered on the dewy grass, the distant sound of flocks and herds on the opposite coast fell on my ears. Then I waked my fellows, and choosing out a few among them, I bade the rest await our return while we set forth in the royal bark to explore the new land on the opposite coast.

The sea was as smooth as a mirror of polished brass. Our oars flew swiftly and sparkled in the sunshine, but old Neptune lay coiled underneath the smooth depths and laughed to himself as we neared the dark coast.

"And now this is positively the last flower-lesson of the season. Remember that we begin again in the autumn. Keep your eyes open, don't forget what you have learned, and bring us 'specimens' of any unusual flower you may come across in your vacation travels."